Anthony Gilbert and The Murder Room

》》 This title is part of The Murder Room, our series dedicated to making available out-of-print or hard-to-find titles by classic crime writers.

Crime fiction has always held up a mirror to society. The Victorians were fascinated by sensational murder and the emerging science of detection; now we are obsessed with the forensic detail of violent death. And no other genre has so captivated and enthralled readers.

Vast troves of classic crime writing have for a long time been unavailable to all but the most dedicated frequenters of second-hand bookshops. The advent of digital publishing means that we are now able to bring you the backlists of a huge range of titles by classic and contemporary crime writers, some of which have been out of print for decades.

From the genteel amateur private eyes of the Golden Age and the femmes fatales of pulp fiction, to the morally ambiguous hard-boiled detectives of mid twentieth-century America and their descendants who walk our twenty-first century streets, The Murder Room has it all. **》》**

The Murder Room
Where Criminal Minds Meet

themurderroom.com

Anthony Gilbert (1899–1973)

Anthony Gilbert was the pen name of Lucy Beatrice Malleson. Born in London, she spent all her life there, and her affection for the city is clear from the strong sense of character and place in evidence in her work. She published 69 crime novels, 51 of which featured her best known character, Arthur Crook, a vulgar London lawyer totally (and deliberately) unlike the aristocratic detectives, such as Lord Peter Wimsey, who dominated the mystery field at the time. She also wrote more than 25 radio plays, which were broadcast in Great Britain and overseas. Her thriller *The Woman in Red* (1941) was broadcast in the United States by CBS and made into a film in 1945 under the title *My Name is Julia Ross*. She was an early member of the British Detection Club, which, along with Dorothy L. Sayers, she prevented from disintegrating during World War II. Malleson published her autobiography, *Three-a-Penny*, in 1940, and wrote numerous short stories, which were published in several anthologies and in such periodicals as *Ellery Queen's Mystery Magazine* and *The Saint*. The short story 'You Can't Hang Twice' received a Queens award in 1946. She never married, and evidence of her feminism is elegantly expressed in much of her work.

By Anthony Gilbert

Scott Egerton series
Tragedy at Freyne (1927)
The Murder of Mrs
  Davenport (1928)
Death at Four Corners (1929)
The Mystery of the Open
  Window (1929)
The Night of the Fog (1930)
The Body on the Beam (1932)
The Long Shadow (1932)
The Musical Comedy
  Crime (1933)
An Old Lady Dies (1934)
The Man Who Was Too
  Clever (1935)

Mr Crook Murder
  Mystery series
Murder by Experts (1936)
The Man Who Wasn't
  There (1937)
Murder Has No Tongue (1937)
Treason in My Breast (1938)
The Bell of Death (1939)
Dear Dead Woman (1940)
  aka *Death Takes a Redhead*
The Vanishing Corpse (1941)
  aka *She Vanished in the Dawn*
The Woman in Red (1941)
  aka *The Mystery of the
  Woman in Red*

Death in the Blackout (1942)
  aka *The Case of the Tea-
  Cosy's Aunt*
Something Nasty in the
  Woodshed (1942)
  aka *Mystery in the Woodshed*
The Mouse Who Wouldn't
  Play Ball (1943)
  aka *30 Days to Live*
He Came by Night (1944)
  aka *Death at the Door*
The Scarlet Button (1944)
  aka *Murder Is Cheap*
A Spy for Mr Crook (1944)
The Black Stage (1945)
  aka *Murder Cheats the Bride*
Don't Open the Door (1945)
  aka *Death Lifts the Latch*
Lift Up the Lid (1945)
  aka *The Innocent Bottle*
The Spinster's Secret (1946)
  aka *By Hook or by Crook*
Death in the Wrong Room
  (1947)
Die in the Dark (1947)
  aka *The Missing Widow*
Death Knocks Three Times
  (1949)
Murder Comes Home (1950)
A Nice Cup of Tea (1950)
  aka *The Wrong Body*

Lady-Killer (1951)

Miss Pinnegar Disappears (1952)
 aka *A Case for Mr Crook*

Footsteps Behind Me (1953)
 aka *Black Death*

Snake in the Grass (1954)
 aka *Death Won't Wait*

Is She Dead Too? (1955)
 aka *A Question of Murder*

And Death Came Too (1956)

Riddle of a Lady (1956)

Give Death a Name (1957)

Death Against the Clock (1958)

Death Takes a Wife (1959)
 aka *Death Casts a Long Shadow*

Third Crime Lucky (1959)
 aka *Prelude to Murder*

Out for the Kill (1960)

She Shall Die (1961)
 aka *After the Verdict*

Uncertain Death (1961)

No Dust in the Attic (1962)

Ring for a Noose (1963)

The Fingerprint (1964)

The Voice (1964)
 aka *Knock, Knock! Who's There?*

Passenger to Nowhere (1965)

The Looking Glass Murder (1966)

The Visitor (1967)

Night Encounter (1968)
 aka *Murder Anonymous*

Missing from Her Home (1969)

Death Wears a Mask (1970)
 aka *Mr Crook Lifts the Mask*

Murder is a Waiting Game (1972)

Tenant for the Tomb (1971)

A Nice Little Killing (1974)

Standalone Novels

The Case Against Andrew Fane (1931)

Death in Fancy Dress (1933)

The Man in the Button Boots (1934)

Courtier to Death (1936)
 aka *The Dover Train Mystery*

The Clock in the Hatbox (1939)

Uncertain Death

Anthony Gilbert

An Orion book

Copyright © Lucy Beatrice Malleson 1961

The right of Lucy Beatrice Malleson to be identified as the author of this work has been asserted in accordance with the Copyright, Designs and Patents Act 1988.

This edition published by
The Orion Publishing Group Ltd
Orion House
5 Upper St Martin's Lane
London WC2H 9EA

An Hachette UK company
A CIP catalogue record for this book is available from the British Library

ISBN 978 1 4719 1018 0

www.orionbooks.co.uk

CHAPTER I

ON the day that Emily Tate vanished, Inspector Marston met her husband on the towing-path of the River Pyle, not far from the weir. Marston had left his car at Chelston for a minor repair and walked the two miles back to Little Wyvern. He was thinking enviously of men who can make their own plans and have a few days fishing when the mood takes them, when he heard something moving in the dense bushes just ahead and a man stepped out on to the path. Stephen Tate was a big fair fellow, handsome in a sober way, and looking little older than when he first came to Little Wyvern at the end of the war, selling insurance. And though he had married old Purdy The Chemist's daughter, Emily, in '47 and stayed more than five years in the neighbourhood before he got transferred to a more important circuit, he was still a stranger to the locals. It occurred to Marston he'd never heard anyone call him Stephen, let alone Steve.

When he found himself face to face with the inspector, Tate gave a start that was almost a jump. Then he recovered and said, 'Not looking for me, I hope,' which was his notion of humour, and Marston said, 'Well, not on a Thursday evening. It's not often we see you here before Friday.'

'That's a fact,' Stephen agreed, falling into step, a bit to Marston's dismay. A nice chap and reliable, but no great shakes as a conversationalist. 'But there's changes in the offing and I wanted to talk them over with Emily. Only, seeing she's not there, I thought I might as well come down to the river, and lucky for me I did. I believe, I really do believe, I spied a golden rambler.'

A man announcing he'd found uranium in his back garden couldn't have sounded more enthralled.

In the country all men have a hobby and river-birds were Stephen's. Everyone knew it; there'd been an unpleasant incident the previous year, when a couple of lads had wantonly destroyed some nests, and Stephen had pitched into them with such violence that one of the fathers had gone to the police.

'A rare species?' murmured the inspector, politely.

'According to St. John Byrne there hasn't been one seen in the south for fifty years. Now, if I could get a colour photo . . .'

Marston wondered what Emily made of the stranger she'd married. The general view had been she was lucky to get a man; thirty at least, and a little tensed-up weasel of a woman, old Purdy's elder daughter and wedded to the business by all accounts. As for him—wanted what was coming to her when the old man died, people said, but when old Purdy handed in his checks nothing changed much, except that they ceased living in the flat above the shop, and Stephen rented The Spinney, and went off every Sunday night to return on Friday as regular as clockwork. Marston, a great family man, thought it wasn't much of a family life for either of them, seeing Emily was in the shop all Saturday; but then they weren't much of a family, just the two of them—like a pair of semi-detached houses, said Mamie Marston, each making allowances for the other—you put up with my wireless and I won't complain if your dog barks, that kind of thing. He thought it was a pretty neat summing-up.

'I suppose Emily wasn't expecting you a day early,' he suggested. 'Probably gone into Chelston.'

Thursday was early closing day in the neighbourhood, but Chelston had a street market that afternoon and a good proportion of Little Wyvern housewives went in on the bus about midday. As good as a club, Mamie assured him, and no subscription.

'Oh, I sent her a wire,' Stephen explained, 'and it's been opened. To tell you the truth, Mr. Marston'—he never gave the inspector his official title when the policeman was off duty— 'it's not just that Emily's out. She's gone. Left me, I mean. And no warning.' He shook his big head, as though he were trying to shake a bandage from his eyes. He sounded utterly bewildered.

Marston was as staggered as if someone had given him a

punch on the nose. Because, though Emily might conceivably leave Stephen, she'd never abandon the shop, which everyone knew was her life, and she couldn't run that from a distance.

'What makes you think she's gone?' he asked at last.

'There was a letter on the table, well, a note really, must have scribbled it in a hurry, didn't sound like Emily. You know how she is, I always say the Day of Judgment'll never catch her unprepared, but this is something I couldn't make head or tail of, about being at the end of her tether and wanting to drive her out.'

'She means you're trying to drive her out?'

'Doesn't make sense, does it?' agreed Stephen. 'I mean, I only keep The Spinney on because of the shop and her having to stay in Little Wyvern. Of course, this was my circuit when we got married, but then Mr. Crouch wanted me to move on and it was a step up, there's no doubt about that; and naturally she couldn't let the shop go. So we came to a compromise as you might say. No, it couldn't be that.'

'Are you sure she's gone?' Marston asked. 'I mean, she might be coming back.'

'In that case why take a bag? All her things are gone from her dressing-table, and her night-things and all. Mind you, she's left a good deal, but then she must have gone in a hurry and I dare say she'll send for them. She hasn't given me any address, but she's bound to write. I mean, there's the shop. She'd never abandon the shop.'

They had reached the gate in the wall leading to The Spinney garden and Stephen surprised him afresh by saying, 'Perhaps you'd come in and take something, Mr. Marston. I don't seem able to understand the situation. I thought a walk might clear my head, but it's obvious something's happened. In fact, I'd take it as a kindness if you would come in for a few minutes.'

Marston thought longingly of the steak and kidney pie Mamie would have in the oven. You could have the Lucullus and the Ritz for him; none of them could turn out a pie like Mamie's. He'd never eaten at either, but he was certain of that. Rich gravy, pie-crust gold as ripe barley and melting in your mouth, mush-rooms for good measure. . . . But though he wasn't on duty he wasn't the man to refuse such a plea. Besides, the whole place was going to be talking about Emily twenty-four hours from now, and it's always advisable for the police to come in on the ground floor.

'What flummoxes me,' continued Stephen in the same careful conversational voice, leading the way round the side of the house to the front door, where the gnomish monkey-puzzler seemed to threaten them, 'is why she didn't stop on and tell me face to face if something was wrong. It's not like Emily to evade issues, she's as direct as a machine-gun; and she knew I was coming to-night, because I found the telegram open on the mantelpiece. I suppose Mrs. Marston wouldn't be able to help?'

He was fumbling for his front-door key as he spoke.

'Well, Mr. Tate, you know how it is,' said Marston, almost apologetically. 'Emily isn't what you'd call a mixer, well, she has the shop and the house and they don't leave her time for coffee mornings or polishing the church brass, and that's where the women meet.'

'I did think last week-end she—well, looked a bit peaky, but you don't do yourself any good saying things like that to a woman. All the same,' he had found the key and was unlocking the door, 'she was brooding, you might say.'

You might say the same of a hen, reflected Marston, following his host into the house. It occurred to him that this was one of the few houses in the neighbourhood he'd never previously visited, not since the old ladies who'd built it at the turn of the century had died and the place had been put up for rental by the heir. There was a big square hall, very neat and polished, with druggeting on the tall stairs rising into the shadows. He hadn't seen druggeting on a staircase in years. There was a dark oil-painting hanging above a good reproduction Jacobean chest—cows? men in armour?—it could be anything in this light—and dark painted doors, all decently closed all the way down to the kitchen at the far end of the house. The polish and tidiness were Emily; the good quality of everything could be attributed to

4

Stephen. The effect was as cold as a church on Saturday afternoon. He thought of his own house, with Mamie's work-basket on one chair and the cat on another, and the *Radio Times* sprawled on the carpet. Home-like, that was the word. There was nothing home-like here.

It was quite a surprise when Stephen opened a door on the right to discover a very modern, highly-waxed cocktail cabinet standing against a wall.

'The boys gave me that when I got married,' Stephen explained, flipping open the catch. 'Emily wouldn't have it in the flat—neither she nor Mr. Purdy drank, not even as medicine—but when we moved here I brought it out. There's whisky or beer, Mr. Marston, whichever you fancy.'

Marston said he'd take a drop of whisky, and Stephen opened a can of beer for himself.

'Here's the telegram I spoke of. Mr. Crouch wants me to take over a new circuit. It's run a bit to seed, chap who had it has started tilting the elbow, that's one of the disadvantages of my line, you have to be a bit convivial'—how he managed it Marston couldn't imagine—'and there was a bit of unpleasantness about a policy, so Ferrers is going to live with his married daughter. It should be a good prospect once it's worked up. Trouble is I don't see how it could be run from Wyvern. Right up north, mean travelling all Friday night and going off again Sunday afternoon. Naturally a wife doesn't marry just to see her husband once a month.'

'Did Emily know about it?'

'It's come up very suddenly. Mind you, Mr. Crouch knew there might be difficulties. "You married men," he said—not that he hasn't got a wife and a quiverful himself—"you've given your hostages to fortune all right." Of course, if Emily hadn't got the shop—but I can't see her parting with that.'

At the mention of the shop there was a change less in Stephen's voice than in the atmosphere, that seemed to drop about a couple of degrees. Doesn't like his wife being independent? Marston wondered.

'I was going to show you that note,' Stephen went on. 'Not

that it says much. Doesn't tell me a thing really about what I could see was on her mind.'

'Did you ask her?' inquired Marston, bluntly. He couldn't imagine being in trouble and keeping Mamie outside.

'I dropped a hint or two, but she ignored them. We had an arrangement not to interfere with each other's professional lives. Oh, it may sound chilly, but these couples that open each other's letters—my parents were like that, and then one day my mother opened an envelope that should have been marked Private, and the next thing I knew I was an orphan and Mother's support for the next ten years.'

'It couldn't be health, I suppose?'

'Now there I did drop more than a hint. "Why don't you go along to Dr. Scarlett?" I asked her. "He might give you a tonic, you're run down." She's like a lot of women, they don't know how to delegate and that, in my opinion, is why so few of the sex ever reach the top of the ladder. Anything they don't do themselves they know won't be done right, and even if they do hand over to someone else they're always on the *qui vive*, and naturally people don't like being watched, they don't like it at all. Still, if it had been something wrong in that direction, you'd expect a wife to confide in her husband, wouldn't you?'

'Well, if it isn't her health perhaps there's something amiss with the shop,' suggested Marston. 'It's a big responsibility. . . .'

'It's what she chose,' retorted Stephen grimly. 'And if that's so you'd expect her to stop on and put things right. Last thing she'd do would be walk out. Oh, here's the letter.'

He handed his companion a half-sheet of paper, written in Emily Purdy's easily recognisable hand; small, cramped yet clear, the words jumped up from the page. 'I am at the end of my tether, I can't go on. Do you want to drive me to desperation? Was that your idea from the first?' And then just her initials.

Marston turned it over. 'Where's the other half?'

'Other half?' Stephen sounded puzzled.

'This is only a bit of a letter. Where's the beginning?'

'That's all there was, Mr. Marston. Emily was as thrifty as a squirrel. You'll find a whole packet of odd half-sheets in her desk, I wouldn't be surprised. Wouldn't you agree she'd written this in a hurry, which looks as though she made up her mind on the spur of the minute. Something must have happened.'

' "Do you want to drive me to desperation?" Does that mean a thing to you, Mr. Tate?'

'Not a thing. I mean, we had our differences, of course, but she knew I was coming, because of the wire. . . .'

'It almost looks as if she wanted to get out before you arrived. Did she take her car?'

'Well, you can't imagine Emily without her car, can you? Like eggs and bacon or fish and chips.' He smiled uncertainly; Marston remained as grave as the Sphinx. 'What bothers me is that Emily wouldn't have parted with the shop whatever happened or she thought she'd found out.'

'What could she have found out?'

Stephen gulped and said, 'It did occur to me you had the idea she'd been led up the garden by someone who thought he might sit in pretty, but she wouldn't let anyone come between her and Purdy's. Even in the old man's day there was jealousy, I couldn't help seeing it. And he knew it, too. Oh, they had their differences. For one thing, he was all against change. "You do as you think best when I'm gone," he'd say, "but the place isn't yours yet." And he'd look at me and give a sort of wink.'

'What did he find so funny?' Marston sounded as gloomy as the Commination Service on Ash Wednesday morning.

'He was old-fashioned, didn't really approve of women wearing the trousers. I've often thought he was so keen on our marriage because he liked to think she'd have a guiding hand after he'd gone.'

'But he left the shop to her,' Marston insisted.

'Well, yes. Yes, he did, Mr. Marston, but by a will that was a dozen years old. I've always believed he meant to make a fresh one and name the pair of us to own it jointly.'

Marston's brows lifted and his face stiffened. 'Did he ever say as much?'

'Well, he wasn't a man ever to say much in a direct fashion, but he'd look at me and tell me, "One of these days, my boy, you're going to want to spend seven nights a week under your own roof." And another time he'd say, "Women are strange creatures. They're loyal and they aren't afraid of work, but you can't depend on them. They take fancies." Mind you, he never particularised, but he came to rely on me in various small ways quite a lot those last two years. Since his illness he got slower, things bothered him. "Come and help me out with these, my boy," he'd say. "All those National Health documents and forms—can't teach an old dog new tricks," he'd tell me. And then he'd want to know what I thought of this or that as an investment. "Never put all your eggs in one basket," he'd say. Emily didn't always like it. "You asked me that yesterday, Father," she'd say, and he'd look at her bland as a cat, and tell her, "Yes, well, now I'm asking Stephen. Don't they say two heads are better than one?" I don't mind telling you, Mr. Marston, it was a shock when Mr. Negus told me there wasn't any will made after I knew Mr. Purdy. Left his younger daughter something and everything else to Emily, lock, stock and barrel. Yes, it was a bit of a shock.'

'If he never spoke of it to anyone else,' began Marston and Stephen said, 'Well, no, not unless he mentioned it to Emily. I've sometimes wondered if he did and she—well, she discouraged him. She'd been at him to have her name over the shop alongside his, but though he had some paper stamped "and dau." he wouldn't go any further than that. He didn't marry till he was forty and then, I've always believed, because he wanted a son to carry on the business, and instead of that he got two daughters. Mind you, Emily was as good as any son would have been, just lived for the shop, nothing was too much trouble. Beattie, the second girl, she was as different as chalk from cheese. A flighty piece, that's how Emily described her, always off on some mad adventure, and surprising everyone by taking George Baynes from the bank in the end. I do hear they're very comfortably settled at Parkville and George has a Jaguar and they take it abroad each summer. You could never persuade Emily to go abroad; one week away at some place where she could get back inside of two hours or so that was her notion of a holiday. Bournemouth or Eastbourne—

she didn't change. Two hours to London like I said and three-quarters of an hour by quick train to Chelston.'

'You didn't help in the shop during Mr. Purdy's time, did you?'

'Well, I had my work.' Stephen looked surprised. 'This wasn't a very important circuit but Mr. Crouch was trying me out. I came out of the Army in '45 and I got the job through luck, got an introduction from a fellow I met in the Middle East, and it wasn't so easy to get young men at that time, not chaps prepared to stick, and it suited me. Then, as you know, I got a step up the ladder to my present circuit. It was awkward in a way because naturally I couldn't work it from home, and a wife with a shop isn't quite like an ordinary kind of wife that can pack up and come with you wherever you go. I suppose she might have put a manager in, but that old Mainprice she kept on after Mr. Purdy died would have let the place go to pieces without her at the helm.'

'Did you ever ask Emily if your father-in-law had spoken of writing you into his will?'

'She says No. Why ever would he seeing I had my own line? And, of course, she was the one that saw him most during his last illness. He'd never been quite his own man since the first stroke he had two years before, didn't come into the shop so much, that's when he took Mainprice on. A stroke of luck for Mainprice, because you'd be looking at a chicken a long time before you thought of him; he and his wife had been bombed out of their flat by a V.2 and he came down and Mr. Purdy took him on. Emily didn't like that, she didn't like it at all. "I'm perfectly able to manage," she said. But it's what I told you earlier, he liked to think there was a man in charge.'

'Didn't I hear a rumour about you managing the shop for Emily?' Marston recollected.

'Well, Emily did mention it, but I've always thought it was against nature for a man to work under his wife. Risky, too. A partner is one thing, but a paid employee, which is all I'd have been, is another. And there's never any knowing how the future's going to turn out. No, if she'd honoured the old man's unspoken wishes that would have been another matter. "You put Tate, late Purdy over the door," I said to her, "and you'll have a partner second to none." But no—"a Purdy built the shop and a Purdy's going to carry it on," she said. "You watch out for Mainprice," I told her. "He's a lazy old devil. Just because he was a good friend to your father you don't have to stand by and watch him drag his feet." '

'Did he?' murmured Marston.

'Well, he wasn't a young man and more concerned with the present than the future, if you get me, just as young Spence, the one she's got now, thinks about the future all the time— his future, mark you—and only uses the present to—to lay a foundation for it. But, of course, she may have been afraid a young chap would try and ride rough-shod, anyway she said Mr. Mainprice had been a good friend to her father, one of the few people he saw during those last few days, and he'd not wanted her to push him out, tortoise and hare kind of thing—and when I took The Spinney she let the Mainprices have the flat over the shop. "At least I know about them," she told me, "don't want a lot of riff-raff wrecking the furniture." '

'They haven't got it now though.'

'Well, Mr. Marston, how could they? They're both dead. Mr. Mainprice went first, had a sort of stroke, very like Mr. Purdy; they wouldn't keep him at The Cottage Hospital, of course, a chronic case they said, so he was sent off by ambulance to Greylands beyond Huntmere, and Louie, that was Mrs. Mainprice, got rooms near by. Must have been lonely for her with the old man away and she knew he'd not be returning. There had been a daughter, but she married an actor or someone and went to South Africa. I always thought old Mainprice didn't like his son-in-law. "She'd have done better to have stopped along of us," I've heard him say. That fellow deceived her something shocking. Putting on a lot of dog, I suppose,' explained Stephen weightily, 'but you know as well as me, Mr. Marston, when a chap's asking a girl to wed he's apt to trim the picture up a bit. And, of course, plenty of men don't like the chaps their daughters choose. I was lucky there, all along the line. You were asking about the flat,' he

10

went on with no change of tone. 'A couple called Hughes have got it. Young Spence didn't want to live over the shop, and anyway it 'ud be too big for a bachelor. It suits the Hugheses all right, one double, one single, like ourselves when we lived there in old Purdy's time. He moved out of his room when we got married, but, mind you, it was his suggestion. Liked the idea of having another man under his roof, I've always thought.'

'About Emily,' said Marston thoughtfully. 'Do you want us to make any inquiries?'

Stephen's eyes rounded in astonishment. 'Why should I? If Emily chooses to go off, well, I didn't buy her like a black slave; and it's a free country. I mean, I was here last week-end and she never said a word about it. It's just that I'd like to know why. Was it sudden? Did she take any money with her? Did she confide in anyone?'

'You didn't think of trying to find out when you found she'd gone?' Marston sounded a bit grim. If it had been Mamie there wouldn't have been one stone standing on another by this time.

'How would anybody know? She'd taken the car—oh yes, the garage was empty, I generally leave my car at the week-ends and travel down by train. Fact is, I do enough driving during the week. It's not like one of those jobs where you go round a Council block collecting burial insurance or anything like that. There's a lot of work attached to it and I cover a good deal of ground, so when I'm back at the week-end I prefer to be on my own feet.'

'There's her sister,' suggested Marston. 'Might she have gone there, if she was in some sort of trouble?'

'What, sooner than talk it over with her own husband? Anyway, she and Beattie were never that close. A flibbertigibbet, she'd say, and she hadn't a good word for George Baynes. A windbag was her word for him. And no, Mr. Marston, I don't think she can be there, because if so the telephone 'ud have been ringing like wedding bells the whole evening, with Beattie dying to tell me what she thought of me. She's got the idea I only married Emily for the shop. But, it's a funny thing, I really do believe I married her as much for Mr. Purdy as anything. I mean, it was the first home I'd ever known. When I was just a young chap Mother and I lived in lodgings, and sometimes she'd do a bit of work, if there was anything in her line going, but of course you remember the thirties, nothing very easy then—and the war and nothing home-like there. Mother died during the war and I came back and got this job and then I met Mr. Purdy almost by chance you might say, and he asked me back one evening. That was the start of it all. After the funeral Mr. Negus said to me— Mr. Negus was the old man's lawyer—"You were like a son to him, Mr. Tate." And that's how I felt, like a son. That's why I felt so badly about not seeing him at the end.'

'He died rather suddenly?' Marston hazarded.

'Doctor had warned us he couldn't last long, though the way Emily went to work you'd think she believed she could defeat God and all the angels. A wonderful daughter, the nurse said— that 'ud be the district nurse, you understand, always thinking of something to tempt him, make him take an interest in things. "You're wasting your time," I'd tell her. "Why not let him go easy without fuss?" I always say when the appetite goes that's the turn of the tide.'

'I always understood she was devoted to her father.' Marston's voice was stiff as buckram.

'Oh, she was a good daughter all right, and there must have been times when she wanted to give him a bit of a push. Well, come to that, I did myself. Once he'd made up his mind he wouldn't budge an inch. The things he wouldn't stock because he thought Our Lord wouldn't like them must have cost him two hundred a year. Emily changed a lot of that when it was her turn, of course, though if you ask me old Mainprice was a bit of a sticker, too. Still, people knew him and that's always important in a chemist's, and he had a way of listening with his head on one side like a blooming canary. I did ask him if Mr. Purdy had said anything to him about the future of the shop and he said, "Well, I did get the idea he was thinking a lot about it, but he never said anything special. Mind you, if we could have got to see him the week after, but he'd gone by then." So many people called and a lot tried to see him and he seemed to want to see them, but Emily had to shut out the neighbours. Mainprice she let through once because the old man was fretting about the shop, and he seemed better, Emily said, afterwards, though spent and tired. And one thing I am sure of, he never realised he was so near his end. Of course he had this heart trouble—he wasn't above seventy-five, and that's no great age nowadays—but he would keep asking Emily how the business was going. I did wonder if he wanted to talk to him to see if the accounts tallied.'

'Oh come,' murmured Marston a bit disgusted, 'is that likely?'

'Emily wouldn't let him think takings were falling off when she was in charge, or of course it might be she didn't want him worried. Anyway he said he'd liked seeing Mainprice and Mainprice said he'd come next week and bring Mrs. M. You remember her, Mr. Marston?'

'I didn't know them as individuals,' the inspector acknowledged.

'She was like his shadow. I don't believe she ever started a sentence after marriage without saying, Mr. Mainprice says . . . I was expecting to see him that week-end—Emily was never much of a letter-writer but she promised she'd send a wire if there was a change for the worse—but he passed away in his sleep on the Thursday night. One thing, I was able to take the burden of the funeral off Emily. She seemed quite stricken, hardly able to sign her own name between the—the bereavement and the interment. I did everything. Old Barkley got the black horses out —say what you like there's nothing gives you quite that choke in the throat as four fine horses with plumes and the black and silver cloths. And Garnet did the refreshments, the best of every-thing, I said, though, mark you, he'd have had every whit as Christian a burial in a pauper's grave on potted meat. But I wanted Emily to have everything the way she liked. Of course, I don't believe in the dead watching or caring if they could watch, but she set great store on everything being just so. We even hired glasses for the port and sherry—I drank port out of a teacup once, Mr. Marston, and believe me, it's not the same thing, not the same thing at all.'

Marston felt like a man under a spell. He'd even forgotten

Mamie's steak pie. He remembered old Purdy, a Sabbatarian, no doubt, but a shrewd old sinner, probably quite capable of spiking his daughter's guns at the eleventh hour.

'I did have a word with Mainprice when it was all over . . .' Stephen was like an electric clock, so long as there's any current it has to go on ticking. ' "Did Mr. Purdy speak of me?" I said. And he told me, "Oh, he liked to think Emily 'ud have someone to fall back on when he was gone." But not a word about me and the shop could I coax out of him, so whether he ever spoke of it or not I'm never likely to know.'

'If he didn't speak of it to Emily or Mainprice and he didn't take any legal steps, why should you think he had the idea in mind at all?' Marston inquired.

'Well, but I don't know he didn't speak of it,' Stephen argued. 'It's not likely Mainprice was going to jettison his job, because I'll be frank with you, Mr. Marston, if I'd been part owner of the shop I'd have had the old boy out on his ear. It wasn't so bad during the war and directly afterwards when petrol was in such short supply and you couldn't get cars; it's a long uphill trek into Chelston and even on a bicycle it's not the sort of journey a busy woman wants to make, but when the buses started running again and transport was easier we'd not have stood much chance with the cut-price chemist in the High Street there and branches of other well-known firms as well. It was a surprise to me Emily wouldn't see it my way, but she said she couldn't throw him out, he hadn't much savings and no family to help, and she said he only had a few years to go to draw the pension and then she could reconsider it, and of course she could throw it up at me that I wouldn't take on the job myself.'

'I've always understood the shop was a very snug little business,' Marston demurred.

'Well, she's got young Spence to thank for that. There's a live-wire for you, almost too much so, and an eye to the main chance, which is natural in a young fellow. And he has a hail-fellow-well-met manner that puts off some of the old folk but the general public appreciates. Takes trouble, too. Always on at Emily to branch out, she said, but she wasn't having any of that. At its present size she could control it herself, but if it got much bigger she'd have to let part of the work go. Well, it's an ill-wind that blows no one any good and Mainprice collapsing when he did gave Emily her chance. Mind you, she treated him generously. Went on referring to him as the absentee manager and paid him part of his salary—just till he could draw the full Welfare State pension, you understand. And even after he went she used to go and see Louie Mainprice. But she was a poor thing, didn't last long after her husband.'

'Everything you tell me,' said Marston, 'makes it seem more improbable that she should just walk out without a word.'

Stephen absently opened a second can of beer. 'You're not drinking your whisky, Mr. Marston.' He began to walk up and down the room, eight steps one way, turn, eight steps back. 'I did think you might be able to help me, being a policeman, I mean. Do you come across many cases of wives just walking out on their husbands for no reason?'

'There's always a reason,' said the inspector firmly. 'It's not always adequate, sometimes it's plain crazy, but it's always there. How about her friends, Mr. Tate?'

'Well, that's another difficulty, I really don't know who they were. When I was down here of a week-end she never asked anyone in—well, that's the only time we were together—and because of our interests being so different, I suppose, I never tried to interfere with the shop after the first—sometimes we'd sit together of an evening and neither of us could find a word to say. It seems ridiculous, but after more than twelve years it was as if everything we'd had to talk about had been discussed already. She didn't care about my job, you see . . .'

'There's one thing you'll have to consider,' Marston told him, delicately. 'The possibility that she was interested in someone else. Women left on their own all the week do sometimes start looking in other directions.'

He got the impression Stephen Tate wanted to laugh but found the situation too grave.

'Not Emily. For one thing, it wouldn't do the shop any good a story like that going around. A chemist's a sort of ally to the medical profession, you might say, and you know what people expect of their doctors. Besides, she hadn't got that kind of nature, I've often thought she married me to please her father as much as anything. If we'd any family it would have been different, I I suppose.'

He seemed to be talking more to himself now than to his companion, sorting out his troubled thoughts like a man conscientiously disentangling a mess of string.

'It's hard to explain what that shop means to her. I don't say she'd commit murder for it—well, naturally not—but anything short of that. I sometimes wonder if she could have endured it if Mr. Purdy had made it a joint affair. It's even crossed my mind that she could have known he wished it but she wouldn't co-operate. Power!' he added after another pause. 'Women care for it more than men, I've discovered. It doesn't seem to matter what field it's in—art or commerce or just men—they need it. It gives them an assurance that Nature hasn't provided, not for women like Emily, I mean. Helen of Troy, now . . .' He fell silent.

'Good lord!' the inspector was thinking. 'If he can do this on two cans of beer!' He was thinking this story wasn't altogether unfamiliar. Not that Stephen had told it before but there had been other men—Crippen, for one, and Sam Dougal and that fellow, Christie, who'd got away with mass murder for years. He pulled himself up sharply. Unless you were a maniac you didn't embark on that sort of thing without a motive, and Tate wasn't mad. Only if there was a motive, Marston told himself, I might begin to have bloody thoughts.

For no particular reason he took the telegram from the mantelpiece. It had been received at Chelston—Little Wyvern had no post office—at twelve o'clock. Presumably it would have been delivered at lunch-time. It had been sent to an address, not a telephone number. Stephen said in his sober unemphatic way, 'Emily's a creature of habit. She never really liked the telephone, though, naturally, I insisted on having one put in. But her father never had a separate one at the flat. He said they could hear the shop ringing, and that was good enough.'

Marston thought they all sounded as though they were creatures from one of the silent films. He had never seen Stephen
hurry, you'd have said his competitors would run rings round
him, yet there was something about that steady ruthless advance
that was compulsive, that could, he thought, be intimidating. The
envelope in which the telegram had been enclosed was crumpled
in the waste-paper basket; it was a neat house, there was no
other scrap of paper or rubbish of any kind there. Moving back,
his foot struck the basket and it overturned, so that he saw the
bit of torn envelope that had hitherto been concealed. Stephen saw
it, too, and with the movement of a man to whom tidiness in his
own home has become a habit he bent down and picked it up.

Automatically he glanced at it and Marston followed his
example. It was part of an envelope that had been roughly torn
into two pieces; the half that Stephen held bore part of a type-
written address. Both men could read it clearly:

> A. M. . . .
> c/o 24 Curt. . . .
> Chelston.

'Does Emily have a typewriter?' Marston inquired, and
Stephen nodded.

'It belonged to old Mr. Purdy and must be nearly as old as he
was. I suggested to Emily more than once she should turn it in
and get a new model, but it was usually a waste of breath suggesting things to Emily. It doesn't do to have shabby equipment, not
in business, it gives the impression you're not doing well. And
of course she never used the machine except for business.'

'Was that typed on hers?' Marston said. 'Would you know?'

'Oh, that's Caliban all right. That's what I call it—Caliban.
You remember, the Monster. See that poor alignment. If I had
a letter typed on that machine . . .'

'Yes, well, that doesn't seem to have bothered Emily,' Marston
interrupted. 'Who's A. M.?'

'I've told you, I don't know her friends.'

'I thought you said she didn't type letters to her friends.'

'That's why A. M. can't be a friend. I expect she was answering an advertisement. New things are always coming up on the market and she'd get free samples. Sometimes she took them up, sometimes she didn't. I know one thing, young Spence would be more adventurous than she is. But she could be making inquiries. 24 Curt—that 'ud be Curtonbridge Street, I suppose.'

Marston frowned. He knew Curtonbridge Street well; it was a narrow lane opening off the Chelston High Street. The police had had trouble there before to-day. Black marketeers had run a very successful racket for a time using one of these inconspicuous houses as a headquarters. He thought that particular line was cleared up, but it was like uprooting weeds. You got rid of one crop and a second sprang up while you slept. It was difficult to connect Emily Tate with anything under the rose, but in his job you soon learned the unwisdom of being dogmatic.

'The only A. M. I ever recollect is old Alice Morrison,' said the voice of Emily's husband. 'She's seventy-five and she lives in The Hollow, and I believe I did hear Emily say they weren't speaking now. She said Miss Morrison took advantage and if she couldn't get her own way she took offence.'

'What did she mean by that?'

'Well, Mr. Marston, you don't need me to tell you there's special opportunities for people in Emily's line. Even in old Mr. Purdy's day he'd get people oiling in and wanting something you could only get on a doctor's prescription. Ready to pay for it, too. Naturally, no one who knew the old gentleman tried that game, but strangers . . . Very specious they were about it. "Oh, Mr. Purdy," one lady said, "you remember those pills you made up for me? Well, I've come to the end of them and I wondered if you could let me have another supply." And it 'ud come out they had some sort of drug in them, and like as not he'd never set eyes on her before. I don't suppose times have changed so much since Emily took over.'

'And you think Miss Morrison . . . ?'

'I wouldn't know. But everyone tells you it's on the increase— what they call tranquillisers, I do know there are some you can't just buy over the counter, you have to get the doctor's say-so. And if this A. M. wrote in and tried to bully Emily . . .'

'That's called blackmail,' said Marston, crisply.

'Mind you, I don't say there's anything like that, I'm just ad-libbing off the cuff, so to speak. But there has been this change in her lately, sort of drawn into herself, and she has gone off, though we don't know for how long. You wouldn't know who lives at 24 Curtonbridge Street, would you?'

'It wouldn't be hard to find out. Quite likely it's an accommodation address. It's not exactly a residential neighbourhood. A few little shops, some warehouses . . .'

'What I don't understand,' repeated Stephen, 'is it's not like Emily to sneak off. You'd expect her to stop and tell me outright, specially knowing I'd be here this evening. No, she must be in some sort of trouble, and I'd be obliged, Mr. Marston, if you wouldn't speak of this. I mean, she's got a perfect right to go away for a few days, if she likes, a bit of nervous exhaustion, say, it's easy to understand. And you know what village gossip is—clack, clack. That's why I don't want a lot of inquiries made and questions asked. She's got a name to maintain here, and she doesn't want to come back and find everyone talking about her.'

'You can't really imagine no one's going to notice she's vanished,' Marston expostulated.

'Well, of course not, but she's a free agent, she's entitled to a few days' holiday. You've known her and the old gentleman for a long time, Mr. Marston, you'd feel like me, want to cover up for her, just till we know how matters stand. There'll be a letter in a day or two, I shouldn't wonder. She won't let the shop run for long, that I do know. And it's like I said, we have this arrangement, we don't interfere with each other.'

'All the same,' snapped the inspector, 'you are her husband.' All this broadmindedness made him sick. Marriage was meant to be cosy, four walls and a roof, shut the door and put up the shutters, and there you were in your private world. The notion of marriage as a prairie swept by all the winds of Heaven made nonsense to him. 'You'll be here for the week-end, I take it,' he added, more coolly.

'I'll be sleeping here, of course, but seeing Emily's gone and not needing me, I might go over to Radford to-mcrrow. They do say the avocet's building there again. They got driven out by barbarians,' his voice hardened when he spoke of his beloved birds as it hadn't hardened when there was some question of his wife being in trouble, 'but they're back at last and now they're a protected species. You know them, Mr. Marston? A lovely bird.' It must have occurred to him that the inspector was looking at him rather oddly, for he broke out, 'I have to make the most of my opportunities. No chance of doing anything in that line during the week, of course, and Sundays Emily likes to have me around. Saturdays she's at the shop, true, but then there's the garden. I had a fancy she might like to work along of me there, women are said to be fond of flowers, but—well, nothing came of that. She doesn't know the meaning of green fingers, and, you can say what you like, but the plants know it.' As if, thought Marston scornfully, they could feel love seeping through a chap's finger-tips, conjuring them up and out of the dark earth.

'Mind you,' Stephen ploughed on, it was a wonder he hadn't gone in for farming or something, 'there's always the chance Mr. Negus might be able to tell us something. He's the lawyer Mr. Purdy had and it was him looked over the papers when I took over The Spinney. She might get in touch in an emergency, but I believe the old man's retired and I fancy I heard her say she didn't think much of the son. For all I know, she's shifted to someone new, there's a very good lawyer in Chelston, I believe, but then she might think he'd talk—no, I know lawyers are said to be as silent as the grave, but with all the new knowledge we have now even graves aren't as dependable as they used to be.'

The voice went on with the monotonous regularity of a train, no emphasis, no passion, no indignation, no grief.

'And in the meantime,' suggested Marston, 'you'll be playing around with—whatever they were you said.'

'There's something about birds,' Stephen explained. 'You and me, we're here to-day and gone to-morrow, a lot of sound and fury signifying precious little, but the birds will still be there when we're dust. That makes you feel small and somehow that's a comfort.' He moved significantly towards the door.

'I must be getting back,' acknowledged Marston. 'Mamie's giving me a treat to-night, and I don't want to go missing too before morning. If you haven't got any news by the time you go back I'd be obliged if you'd let me have a message,' he added. He gave his companion a ferocious smile.

'I'll do that,' Stephen agreed. As they came into the hall his shoe kicked something that clattered a little.

'What was that?' Marston inquired.

Stephen looked surprised. 'Pebble, I suppose. Probably tracked it in on my shoe. There's a woman, Mrs. Rorke, comes to clean once a week—she can attend to that.'

Marston produced a pencil torch from his pocket and turned on the little darting button of light. He identified the object and stooped to pick it up. It wasn't a pebble, after all, but a button, round, silver-coloured, with a bit of material adhering to the shank.

'That Emily's?' he asked.

Stephen took it from him, examining it curiously. 'That's right,' he said. 'She must have been in a hurry not to notice it. It's a funny thing about Emily, always so neat and quick when it comes to calculations and planning, you'd expect her to be—well, deft's the word, I think. But she was clumsy in her own way. Always rushing. Old Slowcoach she calls me. You'll be late for the Day of Judgment, she says. No good reminding her about the hare and the tortoise. The tortoise was a mean cheat and he'd get shown up one of these days. Dashing the way she did she'd lose more time than she'd save, though she didn't like it when I told her so. The numbers of times she's had to open a door a second time because she shut it too quick, caught a bit of her dress. . . .'

He opened the front door. 'I'll put that by, and then if she hasn't matched it up she'll be glad to have it when she gets back,' he promised.

But after he had heard the gate clang behind his visitor he stood for a minute quite motionless, a big block of a man not unlike an Epstein memorial, the same solid strength, terrifying in his immobility. The button still lay in the palm of his hand. He knew it had never come off one of Emily's coats, because, if he didn't notice much what a woman wore, at least this button he could recognise. He knew just whose coat it had come from, and for the first time fear stirred in his breast.

CHAPTER II

ON his way to his own house Marston had to pass the chemist's shop with its black and gold decoration, gold letters on a black ground, and seeing the light from within he pushed open the door and entered. Although it was early closing day the shop re-opened at five-thirty for an hour for the benefit of 'urgent cases' which meant anything from a prescription to a home perm. The shop itself was well situated in the little High Street, between a grocery and Miss Mence's wool-shop, that was temporarily closed, 'owing to the indisposition of the owner.'

Although the light was burning there was no one in the chemist's, but Marston could hear a voice from the room behind. Young Spence was talking on the telephone.

'My dear girl, I assure you it's all tied up,' Marston heard him say. 'Old Emily eats out of my hand. You'll see Spence and Purdy over the door before we're through.'

Marston could imagine the mobile, tanned face, the lips smiling under the short-clipped moustache, eyes ablaze, hands gesticulating though, since we haven't got televisual telephones yet, it might seem a waste of effort.

There was a break there while Darling presumably had her say, and then a sigh deep enough to blow the telephone off the table.

'I tell you, you don't have to worry, you trust Pete,' the man's voice insisted.

The inspector picked up a bottle of fruit salts and set it down with a bang. Instantly the telephone receiver was hung up and young Spence came bounding into the shop like a Jack from its box.

'Why Patience should be a woman's name, search me,' he remarked. He had the sort of face that can give the impression the sun is shining even on a foggy day. 'Well, praise the pigs,' he went on in his uninhibited fashion. (Where on earth had Emily dug up this bright young spark?) 'I thought it was the governess.'

'Mrs. Tate?' Marston's expression was forbidding.

'Govern-or, govern-ess,' explained Peter Spence. 'Well, she was due half an hour ago. Always looks in at six on a Thursday to take the custom while I get ahead with the prescriptions. You know, there's a sort of conspiracy afoot to break your leg or have a hangover on early closing day. Fact, Inspector. More prescriptions on a Thursday . . .' He stopped. 'Am I speaking out of turn? Have you . . . ?' He put out a long narrow brown hand. 'O.K. I'll put you at the top of the list. Always pays to give the police preferential treatment, I'm told.'

'It was Mrs. Tate I came for,' said Marston a bit inaccurately.

'Take a pew. She's sure to be along, though, she's like an electric clock as a rule, never runs down.'

'Except when there's a strike,' Marston suggested.

'You can't mean she's gone on strike? Oh, no. Why, the shop's meat and drink to her as well as bread and butter, and she knows I'm on my own on a Thursday. Of course, there's young Bert, but you can't teach him anything about his rights. "You've cheated me out of fifteen minutes," Mrs. T.'ll say when he drifts along at nine-fifteen. "You stop it out of my pay envelope," says Bert. I say, Inspector, you got anything up your sleeve except your arm?'

'I suppose Mrs. Tate didn't say anything to you about going away for a few nights?'

'What, with the old man coming home to-morrow? That's why she does the accounts of a Thursday, so as to be back bright and early for Mr. Emily Purdy on a Friday evening.'

'Mr. Tate's back,' said Marston in the same considering voice. 'I met him down by the river.'

'That might be the explanation. P'raps he was pushing her in. You couldn't blame him really. I remember a bobby telling me once that most people get themselves murdered through being

24

so vexatious someone or other can't stand it any longer. And, you know, she is enough to drive you up the wall. So pigheaded I wonder she hasn't been picked up by a farmer long ago.'

'That tongue of yours will get you into trouble one of these days,' the inspector warned him.

'I'll come to you to get me out again. No, seriously. You know the shop next door?'

'The wool shop?'

'That's right. Run by an old girl as dotty as the morse code. Well, that's coming on the market any day. Old lady's in the bin and she'll only come out in a box. I told Mrs. T., "Here's your chance. Take a lease and we'll all be on velvet in, say, three years from now." And do you know what she said? "The business won't stand any expansion just now." Can you beat it?'

'If she doesn't want any larger premises,' Marston began, but the young man interrupted indignantly, 'There's others to be considered, there's my future, and Harry, that's the future Mrs. Spence. I tell you, there's a gold mine in that place. Little Wyvern's getting its own share of the tourist trade these days, people going out to Lancet now they've discovered this ancient city, and the new by-pass beyond Huntmere. And what do tourists want? Cameras, of course, photographic equipment of every kind, films developed, picnic stuff. Thermoses—Thermi?'—he looked questioningly at Marston—'postcards—come to that nobody in the village sells them, though the Old Church is supposed to be quite something—we could do a roaring trade.'

'And Mrs. Tate doesn't see eye to eye?'

'She says, "I've got as much as I can handle," but I've got two hands, haven't I? I'd take Bert—he's precious little use in the shop—to help with the developing and all that, she could get someone else here—of course it means a bit of capital outlay, but I'm prepared to pay my whack—I've got some savings and an old auntie left me £500 not long back, and Harry was favoured by Ernie to the tune of another £500—always marry a lucky girl, Inspector—I could run one side of the business and she could run the other.'

'And you can't persuade Mrs. Tate . . .'

'It's Emily Purdy no one can persuade. If you never back an outsider you can't hope to make a packet, and this one would come romping home. Oh, we might have to go slow for a year or two, but she's got a husband to buy her her little luxuries. . . . Oh, she's an aggravating woman all right. Wouldn't surprise me if Mr. Tate did hand her a Mickey Finn.'

'I suppose she knows her own business best,' said Marston, dryly, wondering how he had allowed himself to be inveigled into a gossip of this nature with a young man to whom discretion wasn't even a printed word.

'Mind you,' Spence went on without paying the smallest heed to the older man's advice, 'there'd be plenty of sympathy for him if he did. The way she rides the poor old boy—just let her find out about his girl friend.'

'Did you never hear of the law of slander?' countered the inspector, sharply.

'Didn't know it applied when you were talking to the police. Oh well, p'raps it's his sister really.'

'How long have you been here?'

'As if you didn't know. Four years and a bit. If it was a prison sentence I'd have got remission for good behaviour, but not here. Do you know she doesn't even let me have the key of the poison cupboard?'

'What on earth do you want that for?'

'I do the dispensing, don't I? But no, she keeps it in her petticoat pocket, and hands it over when needed. Honest, I wonder she doesn't ask for a receipt. And now she doesn't seem to realise what she could do, with a chap prepared to work a fifty-four hour week.'

'The place was going a good many years before you came,' Marston reminded him.

'Old Beddoes in the infirmary could say as much, but that's no particular recommendation. Nowadays just being alive isn't enough. You've got to be on the trot twenty-four hours a day. I know what we take over the counter and it could be half as much again with a bit more enterprise. You know what'll happen if she doesn't take up the lease of the wool shop? Some desiccated female with a spiritual twin and well over the century mark between them will open an Olde Englysshe Tea-shoppe. . . .'

'Then being the chemist next door you'll be very nicely situated,' Marston assured him blandly.

'If there's any poisoning to be done we can do it ourselves, and make a profit out of it. Harry's a fine cook. Of course, Mrs. T. knows I can't open up anything in opposition in the same neighbourhood, because that's written into our agreement.'

'You're not tied to Little Wyvern, I suppose.'

'Why should I let her drive me out? I've dug myself in nicely. I never did care for city life. I'd sooner be a big fish in the village pond than a minnow in the ocean.'

'Minnows don't live in the ocean,' returned the inspector, dryly.

'Shows their good sense. Well, anything I can sell you? It's after hours, but the police are privileged, and it don't look as though Madam was coming, after all.'

'When did you see her last?' Marston wanted to know.

'She beetled off round about twelve. Said she'd be seeing me as per usual this evening. Matter of fact, I went round to the house—and there's a museum piece for you—as soon as I'd closed the shop—heard there was something cooking about the wool shop and wanted her to get in on the ground floor, but she wasn't opening any doors.'

'Perhaps she wasn't at home.'

'The car was there, standing outside the garage. Oh well, p'raps she was having a bath. I'll tackle her again in the morning. And now if I don't get on with my prescriptions I shan't have any prospective partnerships, private or professional.'

'If you haven't got the key to the drugs cupboard how can you get on with them?' inquired Marston, sharply.

Young Spence winked. 'More ways into a house than through the front door. A kid could open that if he gave his mind to it. Only that wouldn't occur to her. Lucky really I'm so honest.'

'What does that mean?'

'Now, Inspector, don't come the innocent over me. I could

run a nice little sideline if I were so minded. Dope's worth its weight in gold, and if you're thinking of the Poison Book, well, that can be squared. I dare say Chelston's a cathedral town but that don't mean it's all to the harps and haloes. Shades of Hugh Walpole !'

'I hope you don't talk like this to all and sundry,' Marston cautioned him.

'What do you think? All the same, when you see a chance like this going down the drain and all Madam says is, "Patience can pay good dividends, too," whatever that may mean, well, you do get a kind of fellow-feeling with Vesuvius spraying out all that molten lava.'

The inspector walked thoughtfully homeward; he had learned what he came to find out. Emily hadn't dropped a hint that she might be going away, she hadn't totted up the week's accounts, she had told young Spence to expect her that evening. He was in such a brown study he walked past his own gate, and was only recalled to his senses by Mamie's vigorous knocking on the glass.

'I thought you'd got yourself murdered,' she greeted him cheerfully, coming to let him in.

'Not me,' said Marston, with such a wealth of meaning in his voice that she took his point at once.

'You don't mean—not in Little Wyvern? Well, that will perk things up. Who is it?'

He told her.

'Emily Tate? I shouldn't think anyone would dare.'

'You hadn't heard anything of her going away?'

Mamie said No, and seeing her middle name was Bush Telegraph the situation now seemed to Marston as fishy as a sardine tin.

He said slowly, 'I get the impression that Stephen Tate doesn't expect her back.'

And he added, 'What's more, Mamie, I don't believe I do either.'

And, as if that wasn't sufficient, there was yet another perplexing incident before night. Marston went down to the garage to collect his car and driving back by the river road he glimpsed a point of light on the tow-path. Someone was walking to and fro, flashing a small torch. Marston was about to leave his car, sensing something suspicious about the situation when the man stooped as if lifting something from the ground. As he came closer Marston realised with a shock of foreboding that it was Stephen Tate. Tate gave him a sheepish smile.

'Good evening again,' he said. 'If I hadn't got a clear conscience, Mr. Marston, I should think you were trailing me.'

Now why, thought Marston, should he say that?

'I found I'd dropped the garage key,' Stephen elaborated. 'Must have pulled it out of my pocket when I took out my handkerchief to mark the spot where I saw the golden rambler, and lucky for me I did. The key was there all right.' He held it up with open triumph. 'Never do for Emily to come back and find she couldn't get her car into her own garage.'

'I thought you weren't expecting her back to-night,' suggested the inspector, unsympathetically.

'Well, no, but you know what women are—change their minds as often as they change their clothes—more often than Emily changed hers. Uniform-minded, that's what I used to call her. And she's fussy about that car. You couldn't take more trouble if it was a dog, I tell her.'

'Do you always carry the garage key around with you?' Marston asked.

'Well, there are plenty of light-fingered gentry about, and I keep my tools and bicycle there, and if it's known the place is empty—no, Mr. Marston, I'm not suggesting you'd start such a story, but you know what the village grapevine is, I dare say you mentioned Emily's going to your wife and she might pass it on to a neighbour—so one way and another it seemed best to lock the garage and take the key along.'

Marston thought he'd heard a lot of lame explanations in his time, but this one took the bun. It occurred to him, too, that his companion might be answering some pretty awkward questions in the days ahead, unless Emily surfaced. He murmured something non-committal, and drove off, without offering Stephen a lift.

That same evening a considerable distance away in the village of Periford a girl stood at her window looking out at the night. There was a small moon lying drunkenly on her back, but she didn't see it; there was a freckle of stars and a great white owl rose from behind a wall, jerkily, as though it were a puppet operated by an inexperienced hand. But she didn't see that either. She only saw Stephen's face when she had caught the lapels of his coat a week ago, crying, 'I can't go on, Stephen, I can't go on. I'm going to take Jim Preston. I must do something to break the thread. I'll have a home and children ...'

And Stephen, like a man coming out of a nightmare, saying in a blank dead voice, 'His home? His children?'

'I've got to make a life for myself. You say you can't leave Emily, and she wouldn't give you a divorce. . . .'

'It's you I'm thinking of,' he insisted.

'Men always say that, but if it was true you wouldn't hesitate. Even if it meant your wife making trouble and you losing your job, and you don't even know that for sure, there's always work to be had in the country. You've green fingers, I can cook and clean and sew. We could manage. But that isn't the way you want it.' And then, her head with its dark, silky hair lying against his breast, she had made him promise, 'Tell her this week-end, Stephen. Try and make her understand. It's not as if she were dependent or there were children. I'll tell Jim he must wait one more week.'

He hadn't understood how she could do it, loving him the way she said she did, the way he knew she did. He couldn't have looked at any other woman. 'But you won't leave her either,' she had protested, 'you say you don't sleep together—does that mean you're putting your job, your security before me? Well, what else am I to think?'

The fact was, of course, he wasn't young any more; it's the young who take chances, for whom Hope's a flag that never flies at half-mast. Stephen knew too much, had grown up in the difficult 'thirties, helped to keep his mother till he went into the

30

Army. He'd grown up to hang on to caution like an old woman dragging herself upstairs by a rope ladder, she reminded herself. A shame to blame him. Blame herself rather, for letting it get so far. There's always a place where you can stop if your mind's made up, but once past that you're like a stone rolling downhill. You end over the precipice or in the sea. People would laugh if they knew how she felt about him, but she recognised in her staid lover someone Emily had never met, the young Stephen, buried behind the sedate features, the composed manner, like a youth buried in an ice-floe.

'I feel sometimes like that man who brought a statue to life,' she'd tell him, and they clung together wordlessly, aghast at the miracle of it. When they were together Emily simply didn't exist, nothing could be simpler than to tell her he was going and why not part good friends? It wasn't as though she was in love with him any more, had ever been in love, come to that. Their marriage on both sides really had been more to please the old man than for any other reason, though probably Emily had appreciated the value of being a married woman in a village where spinsters mostly occupied positions below the salt.

But face to face everything changed, his tongue felt as though it had a weight tied on it and blocked his mouth every time he opened it to speak.

'I feel she'll be between us all our days,' Lily had said. She was a simple creature, using gesture as fluently as speech. Her lifted hand touched his heart, and he found the movement unbearable in its confidence and love.

'Lily, I promise,' he said. 'This week-end. I'll make her see. She can't want to hold me when she knows.'

Lily breathed a deep sigh. 'I've never set eyes on your Emily, Stephen, but sometimes I think I know her better than you do.'

'It's not that exactly,' Stephen said. 'It's more—I've had the feeling she was a kind of legacy from her father, a charge. I know it sounds nonsense to you, but I don't believe Emily ever guesses how much she needs someone. But I'll tell her this week-end, I swear I will, my darling.'

But after he'd gone she'd had her doubts. Galahad, she thought, must have been a trial to live with. That was how she thought of him, sober-minded almost middle-aged Stephen, it was enough to make a cat laugh.

The Harmers, John and Mary, were the sort of couple who never expect to see their names in print, quiet people, keeping themselves to themselves, as they say. They had their own house in Little Wyvern, and it was just chance they happened to get drawn into the affair. They slept at the back because it was quieter, and that evening they went to bed a bit later than usual. They'd been watching the telly, they explained presently, a play about a man who killed his unofficial wife and put her body in a wall-cupboard where it wasn't found for years. Usually they were in bed by ten o'clock, but this evening, because of the play, it was after eleven when they closed and locked their bedroom door, a habit they'd formed during the early days of their marriage, when they shared a house and learned you couldn't be too careful. Then last thing Mrs. Harmer drew back the curtains to let in the air.

'That's funny,' she said to her husband, coming back to the bedside. 'Emily Tate's sitting up late tonight.'

Emily was normally like the Harmers, early to bed, early to rise.

'What makes you think she's sitting up?' asked John Harmer, comfortably.

'Light's on in the kitchen. Oh, she's got the curtains pulled, but you can see over the top.' Emily didn't go in for refinements like pelmets. 'Funny place to be at this hour.'

'Love and Bourn-Vita,' suggested John, sleepily. It was one of the advertisements you saw on the telly practically every evening. 'Perhaps she's been viewing, too.'

'They don't have the telly,' said Mrs. Harmer. 'Just the radio—and she's a perfect nuisance with that. I do believe if they had programmes all round the clock hers would never be switched off at all, except when she's at the shop, of course. I don't suppose she listens half the time.'

John didn't think anything more about it then; he was tired

and it was past his proper bedtime. He went peacefully to sleep; but for some reason Mrs. Harmer woke about two hours later and there, to her amazement, was the kitchen light still burning. She wondered if Emily had forgotten—at that stage she didn't know about Stephen's return—but, as she watched, the light went off, and a minute later another one came up on the floor above, and a man crossed the room to draw the curtains. She nearly fainted for an instant, thinking 'Emily? With her husband away at work?' and then she realised it was Stephen come back a day early. They knew all their neighbours' business in Little Wyvern, it was common knowledge that you could set not only your clock but your calendar by Emily Tate. One week's holiday in the year—Bournemouth or some similar watering-place, one year they'd gone as far as Torquay, never went abroad or joined with another couple. Funny about Stephen coming back a day early—she wondered with a little pleasurable wriggle, because life was pretty tame and even a small change in the regular routine promised excitement, if he'd lost his job. It would be something to comment on at the Coffee Morning they were holding for the Summer Outing for Old Folk next day. She didn't guess then that the talk was going to spread a long way further than the Coffee Morning crowd, and that her chance waking at one a.m. might make a whale of difference to Stephen Tate.

She mentioned the fact to her husband next morning, and he agreed it was rum, but he wasn't a woman who can think about two things at once, and his mind was on his job. He had the local grocer's, had inherited from his father ten years earlier, and was ambitious as the old man had never been. And, with competition what it was, you couldn't afford to spare time for speculation about your neighbours, not during shop hours, so he kissed her absently and went off. He scarcely knew Stephen, except by sight, though, of course, they both knew Emily. A good regular customer, thrifty and always knowing where potatoes could be bought a halfpenny a pound cheaper, but paid for stuff on the nail, and bought quality. He'd sometimes thanked his stars he wasn't her husband, but that was as far as it went. He always came back to dinner, as they called their midday meal, and he found Mary in quite a state.

'You remember what I told you about seeing a light at The Spinney?' she declared, excitedly. 'Well, it seems Emily's disappeared.'

John's first reaction was, 'How about the week-end order?' but Mary had gone streets ahead of him already.

'Who told you?' he asked, washing his hands and preparing to sit down to a savoury stew.

'You know Mrs. Rorke? She works there on Fridays, and when she got there this morning there was only Mr. Tate, he told her his wife had had to go away suddenly for a few days, and she was to get on with her usual work. But she hadn't left a note or anything, not for Mrs. Rorke, I mean, and presently, when she was hanging up Mr. Tate's coat, he walked in and snatched it out of her hands. Mrs. Rorke says you never saw anything like his face, and she's sure there were marks on the coat.'

'What sort of marks?' inquired John, phlegmatically. He hadn't been a grocer all these years without appreciating the female love of decoration. They couldn't give you a slice of bread without parsley round the dish.

'Well,' said Mary succulently, 'she thought it could be blood. And he was queer. She took him in a cup of tea, and he was sitting at his desk with a pen and some paper, but he wasn't writing. And there's more to it than that,' she continued, eagerly, helping him to stew. 'He had something in his hand and when she opened the door he turned as if he'd been shot, she said, and put it in his pocket.'

'What was it?' asked John in the same calm voice. 'A gun or something?'

'She couldn't see,' acknowledged Mary, grudgingly. 'But when Mrs. Rorke asked when Emily would be home, he said he couldn't say for certain, she'd write, and for her—Mrs. Rorke, I mean—not to come next week unless Emily's back. Well, you know you can set your clock by her. And that young Spence, he didn't know she was going away.'

'I suppose you asked him,' suggested John, tucking in his table napkin, and thanking Heaven that Mary hadn't forgotten to light the gas under the stew, the state she was in.

'We wanted some more of those bismuth tablets and he was alone in the shop, so naturally I asked, "Where's Emily?" though of course I said "Mrs. Tate" to a young fellow like that, and he said, "Well, don't tell everyone, but she's eloped."'

'These young chaps!' said John, who suffered from them in his own business. 'Nothing serious to them.'

'Ah, but they've had the police round,' cried Mary.

This time she really did engage her husband's attention. 'Who says so?'

'Mr. Marston was in the shop last night, asking if Emily had said anything about going away, but she hadn't because he'd been expecting her, and this is Friday when she always takes the money round to the bank. You mark my word, John, we shall hear more of this.'

'Did you say anything about seeing the light burning late last night?' John inquired, dryly.

'Well, I might have mentioned that there was someone in the house last evening, and he said, "Yes, Mr. Tate came back a day early." And Mrs. Jones, who was there getting a new toothbrush, or so she said, though goodness knows she can't need it, the sort she has, she told us she saw a telegraph-boy—though Joe Masters is fifty if he's a day—coming away from The Spinney about dinner-time yesterday.' And she repeated, 'John, we shall hear more of this.'

Like Mamie Marston, she relished a bit of excitement and why not? We're all going to be quiet enough in the grave. And graves were in everyone's mind and on most people's tongues in the days to come.

At The Sitting Duck that evening Mrs. Rorke, a bony woman with a cast in one eye that gave her a peculiarly raffish appearance, didn't have to pay for a single black velvet, there were so many waiting to treat her. She was the one person—if you excluded the inspector and at that stage no one seemed to know about his call at the Tate homestead—who'd been inside the

House of Mystery and she told the story of Stephen Tate's extraordinary appearance, like he'd seen a ghost, she said, so often that what had started as a mere caterpillar of surmise ended as a great booming moth of conviction. By the time Sam Henderson was calling, 'Last Orders, Gentlemen, Please,' everyone was pretty sure Emily Tate wasn't coming back to Little Wyvern, not of her own free-will anyway, and for once public opinion was right.

CHAPTER III

STEPHEN found no letter from his wife in the box that Friday morning so, when Mrs. Rorke had done her worst and departed, he got out his bicycle and went over to Radford. Emily's story hadn't reached there yet, and he had a quiet afternoon tracking down the breeding ground of the avocets, but when he returned about seven o'clock, having had a quiet drink at the Radford Arms, where he wasn't known, he found a number of people hanging about near The Spinney, staring at the house's blank idiotic face as though it were a free Chamber of Horrors. When they saw him they melted away, all except young Eastham of the local *Gazette*, who came up, bold as brass, to ask Stephen if he had any statement to make.

'Statement about what?' demanded Stephen, woodenly. 'Don't tell me your rag's interested in the avocet.'

From the blank look on his face it seemed improbable that young Eastham knew what an avocet was.

'Well, there's talk in the village that Mrs. Tate's gone away,' Eastham said.

'Any reason why she shouldn't?' Stephen wanted to know. 'This isn't a country behind the Iron Curtain, people can go off for a few days if they've a mind.'

Of course, an English village isn't like a town. People are still individuals, not units. When Miss Armstrong's old mother won £500 in the Premium Bonds that was news, and when Major Hardy's Alsatian won a prize at the County Show he and the dog were represented by a photograph; true, it came out so muzzy that it was all odds which was dog and which was man, but they say that those who live together tend to grow alike.

'You must be hard up for news,' said Stephen, and though his voice was quiet enough there was such a strength of fury behind it that the young man shrank back. No one could call him timid, but there's no sense sticking your neck out too far.

'Well, she might have gone into hospital, and as one of our leading citizens she'd merit a paragraph,' he said as jauntily as he could.

'She's gone away for a few days,' said Stephen. 'You can make what you please of that, but, if you take my advice, you'll sing small. She won't be pleased to know you're keeping tabs on her every movement. It's a pity you've nothing better to do than stick your nose into other people's affairs.'

'I hear Mr. Marston was up here last night,' persisted young Eastham with a courage that, in a war, might have won him a decoration.

'That's right. He had a drink, too. Print that if you want to. There's nothing to stop a policeman having a drink, I suppose, when he's off duty.'

He went into The Spinney and slammed the door. This was the beginning, he thought. The telephone rang twice that evening, but he didn't answer it, but when someone came calling and wouldn't go away he had to open the door. It occurred to him it might be Marston back, but it wasn't, it was young Spence looking trim enough to be attending his own wedding.

'Sorry to disturb you, Mr. Tate,' said the young man. 'I wondered if you could give me any idea when Mrs. Tate will be back. There's the money to pay in, you see, and, though she always does it herself, now she's not here I don't like to leave it on the premises over the week-end.'

'Then you'd best pay it in in the morning,' Stephen told him. 'You're her manager, aren't you?'

'Whatever you say,' Spence agreed. 'She didn't happen to mention she wouldn't be in last night. I thought maybe she'd had an accident.'

He'd done a better trade than usual that day, so many busy-bodies dropping in to find out what he could tell them, which was precisely nothing. Still, he knew his onions, he didn't let the sharpest of them get away without buying something, whether they wanted it or not. And if they proved intractable he referred them to Stephen. 'I'm not her husband,' he pointed out. 'She doesn't confide in me.'

They could believe that all right. Very head-in-the-air, nose-in-the-sky, that was Emily Tate. The bolder among them were already wondering if she was still sticking her nose in the air somewhere—some lonely part of the woods, say, on the other side of the river. They'd already decided one thing, that wherever she was now she hadn't gone there of her own free-will.

It lent a delightful tinge of excitement to a fairly monotonous existence; they were more grateful to her than they'd been in a dog's age.

Sunday morning the milkman rang the bell of The Spinney, an unheard-of thing, since that's the day most people take a long lie-in.

'About the milk, Mr. Tate,' the milkman said. 'Do you want it left to-morrow? Mrs. Tate didn't say anything about stopping it.'

'She went off in rather a hurry, but—no, don't leave it any more till further notice.'

There was a bit of slate and a pencil by the back door on which Emily dotted down her requirements for the milkman and baker, and he left a message cancelling the bread, too. It had rained on Saturday night and the garden glittered with emerald weeds. He thought he might as well spend his time dealing with them. And he went round sweeping up the mud he'd brought in on his shoes. After lunch he called it a day, and sat indoors, drawing the curtains early, and since there was no pet animal to be put out or exercised he couldn't have told you if anyone was watching the house or no.

He was off on Monday before the post came in, but he knew there wouldn't be anything from Emily; he stopped at the police station to leave a message for Marston.

'No news,' he said briefly. 'He'll understand.'

'Word of six letters meaning violent departure,' quizzed one of

39

the younger constables. (This was Chelston, not Little Wyvern where a Sergeant Higgs kept law and order or supposed he did.) Stephen drove into Pembury, the centre of his district where he'd parked his car, and from the post office he sent a telegram to a girl called Lily Vane.

Expect me to-night. Important development, it read. It wasn't signed. He knew there was no need.

It was a good day, in spite of its beginning, and he netted a client for his company that two other firms were after. Nobody seeing him would have thought there was anything different from usual. He made the same sedate jokes, listened with flattering sobriety to other men's tales, had two drinks at The Turtledove, and then got into his car and drove to keep his rendezvous. It was almost an hour's drive and the dusk was low on the hills beyond the town, but the village where he stopped might have come off a Christmas card. Lily's cottage overlooked a green with a pennyworth of water and three white geese; there was a pub on the far side and a seat outside it where the old chaps sat around till opening time. The landlord of The Bull of Basan knew it paid him to let them hang about, they were where he wanted them as soon as the clock struck.

Lily was waiting at the window for her lover; before Stephen could ring the bell the fairy-tale door opened, two arms came into the darkness and drew him within. Like the sirens, he thought vaguely, drowning in their close embrace. She wasn't much taller than Emily, but there the resemblance ended; she was dark, a spirit of night, he thought, dusky hair, grey eyes, where Emily was mousy with hazel eyes as hard as nuts. And her hands were gentle and compelling, where Emily's held and maintained and never opened to let a thing go that could have the smallest value for her.

'You're late,' whispered Lily. 'Oh, you've died a hundred times in the past year. Did you ever think, my darling, you could be ill, dying even, dead and buried and I'd not know except by chance. Who would there be to tell me?'

'Hush!' he said. 'I'm not going to die yet awhile.'

She took him into a little low-ceilinged room, with blue curtains hanging at the windows, and when she had drawn these a pot of rosy hyacinths sprung up like a light in the dusk.

'Stephen, what's happened?' she asked. 'I got your wire when I came in. You've told Emily? What did she say?'

'Sit down, Lily,' he said, tenderly. 'I've got a lot to tell you.'

'I see.' Her voice was as quiet as his. 'You mean, it's no good. She won't give you a divorce.'

It wasn't a question but a clear statement of fact. He said in the same quiet voice, holding her close, 'What made you go and see her? I could have told you it was the last thing to do.'

'So she told you? Yes, I suppose she would.'

'What made you go?' he repeated.

'Are you angry with me? I thought if we met, two women, I might make her understand. Thursday was my free day last week'—(she worked in a hotel and they all did Sunday rota which gave them a weekday every fifth week)—'so I bought a day ticket and came to Chelston. I knew being early closing day she wouldn't be in the shop, so it seemed likely she might be at home. I found the house quite easily, and I rang and first I thought she wasn't going to answer. I could hear voices and then I realised she had the wireless going.'

Stephen nodded. 'That's right. She likes the wireless, company, I suppose.'

'I rang a second time, because I knew she must be there. If she hadn't come I'd have waited all the day or—or broken a window or something, I had a desperate feeling, this was our one chance, everything depended on me. At last I suppose she realised I wasn't going away, she came into the hall and jerked the door open just a little way. "What do you want?" she said. I said, "Mrs. Tate, I'm Lily Vane. Stephen may have spoken about me, if not, he's going to tell you this week-end. We love each other . . ." I saw she was staring, so, of course, I knew she didn't know.'

'I told you I was going to tell her.'

'I thought I could spare you, if she knew already . . .' She shook her head and turned closer towards him.

'What did she say?'

41

'It was horrible. She can't have been back long, she was still in her outdoor clothes. She said, "Get out, you slut." '

Stephen gave a start. He hadn't believed that Emily would agree to his plan, but somehow he hadn't anticipated such fury.

'She wouldn't let me come any farther, I'd just got over the threshold. When I tried to explain she caught me and shook me and said, "Get out, you've no right in a decent person's house." I've misjudged you, Stephen. I've been thinking, "If he wasn't a coward he would tell her." I didn't know what she was like. I could see, of course, it was no use. Oh darling, what made you marry her?'

'I suppose because I wanted a home, something I hadn't had since I was a boy. It was more than getting a wife, though I wanted that, too, it was finding a background after years of drifting in rooms and then the Army, no family, no ties. And I was fond of the old man. And how could I guess I was ever going to meet you! At my age no man could know that would happen. Even now I can scarcely believe it. To walk into the Rose and Crown because the Pig and Popgun was being painted, and to find you there behind a desk. And, you know, it worked very well for a time. We were good friends anyway till the old man died. Then things changed. It wasn't only that I didn't get my share of the shop, it was something in Emily. Perhaps she made me realise the shop mattered more to her than I did. Not that it would have made any difference once I'd met you.'

'I never even stopped to wonder if you were married,' Lily recalled. 'People should have some warning.'

'Go on,' Stephen bade her gently. 'What happened? How long were you in the house?'

'Just a few minutes. I could see it was no good. I did try. I said, "You can't help love, it happened before either of us could stop it, and now it can't be undone." She—she tore a button off my coat.'

'I know.' He put his hand in his pocket. 'I've got it here. Sew it on to-night, Lily. And promise me something.'

'Anything. Anything. Oh, Stephen, I'll come away with you or go on as we are, whichever will hurt you least. I didn't know any woman could be like that. The things she said! I could have murdered her.'

'Never say things like that. It doesn't become you. Now, think carefully. Did you tell anyone you were coming to Chelston?'

'Of course not.'

'Have you said anything to anyone since?'

'No. I haven't seen anyone, not really to talk to. I couldn't talk to anyone at the Rose and Crown.'

'You might let it out by chance, that you were on the train that day, I mean. You must be careful, Lily. You might be tricked into saying it.'

Her grey eyes widened. 'Stephen, I don't understand.'

'Never mind. Did anyone see you go up to the house?'

'No. No, I'm sure they didn't. There was no one about. It was lunch-time, you see.'

'It's always quiet there. You're sure there was no car or bicycle?'

'I don't think so. I did look round because I wasn't quite sure of my direction, but there wasn't anyone to ask.'

'And no one saw you leave?'

'Again I don't think so, but everything was a mist by then; I dare say I wouldn't have seen a double-decker bus.'

'How did you get back to the station?'

'I walked.'

'Walked? It's all of two miles.'

'I wouldn't have noticed if it had been twenty-two. Stephen, what did she say about me?'

'You don't need me to tell you. Lily, I've got a plan. Mr. Crouch wants me to take over a new district, in the north, that's run to seed a bit. "I daresay it'll depend on Mrs. Tate," he said. When I rang him up this morning I said I thought I'd managed to persuade her to let me take the job, so now everything depends on you.'

'You mean, me and you?'

'It's a strange neighbourhood. No one's ever seen Emily, and, what's more important, we shan't meet anyone who knows anything about her. You can be Mrs. Tate, no reason anyone should know . . .'

'Emily will know. Emily won't let you go so easily.'

'You don't have to worry about Emily. She's left me. Oh yes, that's my news. There was a note on the table when I got back, and some of her things were gone.'

'But, Stephen, you always said she wouldn't leave the shop.'

'Young Spence will watch her interests. She won't be back so long as I'm at The Spinney, that I do know. And when I leave it won't be of any importance to us.'

'But—the divorce?'

'We may not be able to get that yet, but she won't come up north and make trouble. She has her own reputation to think of. I've written to her, care of Mr. Negus, and if he doesn't know her whereabouts I'll try again through her bank. She might not write to me, but she must write to them. Oh, Lily, I know this isn't the way we hoped it might be, but life's mainly a matter of compromise, and who are we to escape it?'

She sat very still for some time, his large hand folded between her two narrow ones. At last she said. 'Stephen, what haven't you told me? Have you made some bargain with her? I can't believe she'll let you go like this.'

'You're prejudiced,' he said: 'Most women don't want to keep a reluctant husband, and she has her own business. I can make arrangements about money later on.'

She said in the same muted voice, 'If it's going to hurt you, you know I'd sooner die.'

'Don't speak of dying.' The pain in his voice was as rough as a nettle-sting. 'I dare say she won't write to me direct,' he added carefully. 'But I shall hear any developments there are. I'll go down to The Spinney again next week-end. I dare say things may have moved a bit by then.'

'When shall I see you again?'

'I'll let you know. But in the meantime, don't write, don't speak to anyone. There may be a bit of unpleasantness, that's only to be expected. Oh, you might give notice to Mr. Davies. Tell him some story, you're going north to join your sister or something. Better not say you're getting married. They'd ask too many questions.'

'And we're not,' she reminded him, simply.

'One day,' he promised. 'One day.'

Presently he said reluctantly, 'I mustn't be too late back, don't want to find the hotel locked against me.'

He kissed her as though he'd never let her go. 'Remember what I told you. I want your name kept out of this. At any cost, Lily, at any cost.'

Only, for all those brave words, he must have known that wasn't going to be possible.

Oh yes, he must have known even then.

CHAPTER IV

H E was busy clearing up business all that week and he didn't arrive at Little Wyvern until midday on Saturday. It could have been his imagination, but it seemed to him there were eyes at every window. It had been a dull morning and by one o'clock storm clouds were lowering. The letter-box at The Spinney was stuffed with envelopes. Mrs. Rorke hadn't been in, of course— Emily would never give her a key but waited till she arrived on Fridays, then took the money to the bank and came back about twelve o'clock to pay the woman off. It seemed strange that so careful a woman should be in such a jam. Stephen glanced through the letters, noting a similarity in most of them. They came in cheap envelopes, were crudely addressed, and their contents were cruder still. There were so many of them that the postman had had to push some under the door. The only letter for Emily was his own, returned from Mr. Negus's office. Methodically he re-addressed it care of her bank at Chelston. Then he began to sort his own mail. Some of the writers openly accused him of having done away with his wife, others merely posed questions.

What were you doing in the kitchen at one a.m.?

He was staggered at their knowledge. Others were simply obscene rubbish. He knew, of course, that you should take anonymous letters straight to the police, but that would bring Lily into prominence.

He carried the letters into the garden where he burned them—carefully in an old enamel plate and blew the ashes far and wide. Then he went back to the kitchen and brewed himself a cup of tea; the rain that had begun to spatter the windows now started to come down in earnest and within twenty minutes it was a deluge. It came down in clouds and torrents, as if it would sweep the house away. Standing as it did in its own grounds, The Spinney seemed curiously unprotected. Stephen dealt with some work he had brought back with him and then tried to settle to a book, but it was no use. He saw Emily everywhere and behind Emily the ghostly figure of the girl he now loved. At about four o'clock he went round drawing curtains to shut out the darkness and the rain. The monkey-puzzler, swaying in the wind, seemed to block every fragment of the remaining light from the dining-room where he was sitting. The solitude soon began to pray on his mind. For, though he might know himself to be alone, the house appeared haunted by a secret life. The furniture uttered the loud unexpected groans of ancient wood, a door creaked open, a board cracked as if an invisible foot passed over it. When he leaped up to close the door he started, as though someone had laid a hand on his shoulder, but it was only one of the innumerable heavy curtains that enclosed the house like a tomb, swinging forward to touch him as he passed. He remembered that he had told Mr. Crouch he could probably start on his new round at the beginning of the following month. Now he began to wonder whether he could, in fact, spend another weekend alone in this house of memories.

The clock moved on, the rain continued to fall. The silence of the house, apart from those eerie creakings, began to depress his spirit beyond endurance. Emily had always refused to have a television set, but she had been a radio fan, having the thing going all through the day. There was a small transistor set in her bedroom, remembering which he climbed the stairs to bring it down. He put on both bars of the electric fire, rattled the dark curtains along their wooden pole, switched on the light and set the radio in motion. The music instantly rang through the room, bright as daylight, compelling as a bell. It brought back memories of a sunlit world, and insensibly his dejection began to lift. He carried the set with him into the kitchen when it was time to make the evening meal, and later still he carried it with him up to bed.

By next morning the rain had cleared, though the garden was in a sorry state. He had promised himself a long riverside walk, but the tow-path would be inches deep in mud; that was the reason he gave himself for staying at home, but in his heart he knew he couldn't face the prospect of some casual encounter during which Emily's name was bound to be uttered. He thought he might put in some useful work tying up plants and clearing the branches that had been blown down in the gale, but, if he was prepared to ignore the world, it had no intention of leaving him alone. He had just pulled on his heavy garden boots when the front-door bell rang and there was Marston on the step.

'I heard you were back,' said Marston, making no apology for this Sunday morning call. 'I wondered what news you had of Emily.'

'Nothing,' Stephen told him, woodenly.

'Have you considered the possibility of accident?'

'If there'd been an accident we should have heard. Emily would have her driving licence and her purse, I should have been notified. If Emily gets into any sort of jam she knows she's only to contact me, and she hasn't done so. I don't propose to hound her. I can only repeat my assurance that she left no clue in this house as to why she should go so precipitately.'

He got rid of Marston quite quickly, and went out to the garage to collect his spade and a basket. Working in the moist air calmed his nerves; there was a good deal to be done, he even managed some digging in the piece of ground he had reclaimed and tried to turn into a kitchen garden. It hadn't been a very successful venture, he had had no co-operation from Emily, who was as happy eating shop or tinned vegetables as fresh-grown ones, and didn't care about flowers in or out of the house. And it had proved almost impossible to get a gardener to come up to the house, since Emily wouldn't give anyone a key.

At lunch-time he came in, tracking a good deal of clogged mud on his boots, and stood in the little passage by the back door, scraping it off with a spade. After he had eaten he decided to write to Lily and tell her what he had settled with Mr. Crouch, but everything seemed against him. He had penned no more than a couple of lines when someone rang the front-door bell.

'That harpy, Mrs. Rorke,' he reflected, 'or young Eastham from the local *Gazette*.'

'Ring away,' he said savagely.

The visitor wasn't so easily discouraged. When no one answered the bell he began to tap incessantly on the window-pane—tap, tap, tap, like a woodpecker. Stephen rose, pulled a sheet of blotting paper over the letter he had just begun and stormed into the hall.

'There's no one at home,' he began, opening the door a few inches, and then stopped dead at sight of the pretty, greedy face of his sister-in-law, and her jolly rocky-looking husband.

'Surprise, surprise,' said George Baynes, buoyantly. 'If you want to give the idea the house is empty you should switch off your electric fire. You can see the glow through the curtains.'

Stephen stood back reluctantly to let them in; Beattie looked about her in amazement, her nose wrinkled. The house had the deplorable appearance of all neglected interiors, dust lying on the furniture, the door handles smeared, the tiles bordering the rug greasy and unpolished.

'What on earth's going on?' she demanded. 'Is Emily ill?'

'If you'd rung up you could have saved yourself the journey,' retorted Stephen ungraciously. 'Emily's gone away for a few days.'

'Where?'

'If she didn't write and tell you . . .'

'That's just the point, old man,' broke in the buoyant George. 'She's missed the little woman's birthday first time ever, and Beattie would have it that something was wrong. If you ask me,' he winked at his brother-in-law, 'I believe she thinks you've knocked her on the head and buried her among the 'taties.'

He was a great joker, was George Baynes, could keep the bar in a roar any night of the week.

'She's gone on private business,' said Stephen. 'You know, I never interfere with her movements. I'm sorry about the house, but the fact is Crouch wants me to take over a new district that's run a bit to seed . . .'

'Why should you accept?' Beattie demanded. 'Do we have to stand in the hall all day?'

'Of course not.' He led them into the dining-room. The drawing-room might have been better, but there was no fire there, and probably the dust was even thicker. Not that the dining-room had a particularly welcoming aspect. The ash-trays were full, there were newspapers on the floor, a used glass on the chimney-piece.

'Anyone can see you're lacking the feminine touch,' observed Beattie with simple brutality. 'What about that slut, Mrs. Rorke?'

'She didn't come this week.'

'I always told Emily the woman was no good.'

'Emily seemed to think she was all right. She couldn't come this week because there was no one here to let her in. I shall leave a key somewhere for her to come and clean up to-morrow.'

All this while Beattie was standing expectantly in the middle of the floor.

'Aren't you going to sit down?' asked Stephen, helplessly. 'What about your coat?'

'What about it, old man?' boomed George. 'That's the point.'

For the first time Stephen saw that his sister-in-law was wearing a smart little fur jacket in what was called platinum mink.

'George's birthday present to me,' smirked Beattie. 'You should give Emily a fur coat some time. It does wonderful things to a woman.'

George beamed. It was a good bit of fur and a bargain, trust Georgie. He always knew a man who knew a chap, and the result was always the same. George Baynes got what he wanted—or what his missus wanted—at bedrock prices. It seemed to increase the value of the article.

Stephen admired the coat, helped to take it off and hung it over a chair in the hall. He supposed he'd better offer Beattie tea.

'I'm afraid there's nothing much to go with it,' he apologised. 'Perhaps George would rather have a drink.'

'Now you're talking,' said George.

'It's not four o'clock,' exclaimed Beattie, looking shocked.

'Any time's drinking time,' said George fatuously.

'What brings you here anyway?' Stephen asked.

'Well, I guessed something must be wrong with Emily that she hadn't written, so I said to George, "You can just take me to lunch at the Royal Ascot and then we'll go on and call at The Spinney."'

Even in the whirl of dismay in which he was engulfed Stephen noticed she hadn't though of inviting him and Emily to lunch with them. George did pretty well, was clever at putting out his money at interest, better off than Stephen, most likely, but he expected it to earn him dividends, and there was nothing to be got out of the Tates.

'You must know where she's gone,' Beattie insisted. But he said, No, she'd gone very suddenly and left no address. She'd taken a suitcase and the car. . . . Even George began to look a bit grim at that.

'Do you mean she's left you?' demanded Beattie in her outspoken way.

'You know as much as I do. I came back and found a three-line scrawl saying she was going away. No more, no hint where she was going or when she'd be back.'

'Have you been to the police?'

'It happened that I ran into Marston that evening and of course I told him. . . .'

'Can't they do anything?'

'I haven't asked them.'

'Why not?'

'I don't regard Emily as a missing person, and she won't want to see her picture in all the papers.'

'Here, I say, old man,' burst in George with a kind of heavy roguishness, 'what have you been up to? I always thought the old girl was pretty trusting. . . .'

'Oh, do stop it, George. Don't talk such nonsense. Emily wouldn't walk out and leave the shop and everything because she thought Stephen was carrying on with another woman. She'd have had it out with him. Where's that note you told us about?'

'I must have a gramophone record made,' said Stephen with

a suppressed savagery that made old George sit up. 'My wife has gone away without notice, I do not know where she has gone or when she will be back. I don't know what arrangements she has made about the shop, because the shop is no concern of mine. And it's no use going round to see young Spence, because he knows no more about it than I do.'

Even George began to realise the situation was as fishy as Billingsgate.

'Don't you think you should put out some inquiries?' he suggested.

Stephen turned away towards his cocktail cabinet and began to mix drinks.

'All this talk I'd forgotten I was host,' he said, bringing George a glass and a syphon. 'What inquiries do you suggest?'

'You could find out from the bank if she'd taken any funds.'

'The bank wouldn't tell me. One thing, her passport isn't in her room. She may have gone abroad.'

'Good lord, old man, you're not suggesting she's gone off with another—not Emily?'

Stephen hesitated, then told them about A. M.

'And don't ask me who he is, because, again, I don't know.'

'You mean, you haven't a notion . . .'

To their amazement Stephen suddenly began to laugh. 'What's so funny?' Beattie demanded.

'Do you remember that joke your father was so fond of? What did Neptune say when the sea ran dry? I haven't an ocean.'

George gave a sort of giggle. Beattie was furious. 'I'm going to the police,' she said.

'Here, hold on,' counselled George. 'Em's free, white and goodness knows she's over twenty-one. If anyone goes to the police it should be Stephen.'

'Three rousing cheers,' approved Stephen, heavily. 'I'll see to that kettle.'

'If she's gone to ground,' began George, and his wife sent him an odd glance from her long, half-closed eyes.

'That's a sinister thought.'

George stared. 'Oh come, old girl, don't let's go all melodramatic. Emily always was a bit of a mystery. Fact is, of course, she and Stephen have had a few words, and she's gone off in a huff. When she thinks he'll be in a real lather she'll come swooping back.'

'And have the whole place speculating whether she's been in a lunatic asylum or something? Of course she won't.'

'Now that's an idea,' persisted George. 'Nervous breakdown. Amnesia perhaps. She always worked for two.'

Stephen, who had been clattering about in the kitchen, now came in carrying a pot of tea.

'That kettle never boiled,' Beattie accused him. 'There'll be bits floating all over the surface.' She looked distastefully at the cups that didn't match their saucers and the kitchen tray of black tin with a chipped rose in the centre.

'Or, of course,' continued George, who was a trier and no mistake, 'she might be having a last trot round the paddock. She must be rising fifty' (Beattie, who liked to pass for forty and was only four years her sister's junior, sent him a look of hate), 'it's a dangerous age when women crave for romance. It's a fact, dear,' he added quickly, as his wife prepared to deal him a backhander that would knock him into the middle of next week, 'there was Camille Holland, remember.'

'Someone else out of your murky past?' demanded Beattie, tartly. But Stephen knew.

'A respectable elderly spinster who fell for a loud-mouthed cad ten years her junior, and threw up everything to go with him to a lonely farm.'

'And got herself murdered, because she wouldn't let him handle her money.'

'And that's what you think has happened to Emily? Charming. Only I don't agree with you.' And then she said it, electrifying both men and freezing one where he stood, 'I don't believe Emily ever left this house.'

'Don't take any notice of her, Stephen,' advised George hurriedly. 'She doesn't know what she's saying.'

'If she's gone,' Beattie continued, 'why has she left that behind?' And she pointed accusingly to the little transistor set on the side table.

'Well, why on earth not?' Stephen demanded. 'If you want to get out in a hurry, don't ask me why, you don't stop to think about a wireless.'

'Emily would. She couldn't imagine the day without one. She even used to have it in the bathroom, she told me. Stephen, I'd like to see my sister's room.'

'What for?' asked Stephen, staring.

'Is there any reason why I shouldn't? It's not your room, too, I gather.'

George turned red, Stephen went white. He crossed to the desk and fished out a key.

'You keep the room locked?'

'I told you, I intend to give Mrs. Rorke a front-door key to get the place cleaned up. I don't want her rooting among Emily's private things. I don't even know how honest the woman is.'

'It's quite astonishing, the number of things you don't know,' agreed Beattie, snatching the key and marching out of the room.

As they heard the room above being opened George, all gravity now, turned to his brother-in-law.

'Nothing you'd like to tell me, old man?'

Stephen automatically replenished the empty glass. 'Such as?'

'Well, it's a thin story. Emily wouldn't have walked out just for a joke. Matter of fact, she hasn't any sense of humour.'

'Even I had penetrated that.'

'Talks like a lexicon,' thought George, feeling offended. From overhead came the sound of drawers being opened and shut with a peculiarly irritating clash. You'd almost think Beattie expected to find her sister in the wardrobe, and for all Stephen knew she did.

'You should have told us, you know,' said George. 'It's going to look damned odd when it comes out.'

'When what comes out?'

'That Emily's disappeared.'

'But everyone knows that. What none of us know is why.'

'Sooner or later you'll have to satisfy them,' said George.

'Emily hadn't been herself lately, she's got something on her mind, but she never talks to me. If there was any trouble—only it's unlike her not to stay behind and face the music. . . .'

The door opened and Beattie came back. 'If Emily packed her own case she must have done it in the dark or with her eyes shut,' she snapped. 'Half the things she'd need she's left behind. And the state of her drawers—well, you know she was always as neat as a new pin.'

'Perhaps she packed in a hurry,' George offered.

Stephen said, 'Are you sure there's nowhere else you'd like to look? How about the garage?'

'Stephen's joking,' said George uncomfortably, but Beattie flashed them a defiant look.

'Why not?' she said. Without a word Stephen opened the door.

'You're sure that's not locked, too?'

'Of course it is. But I have the key. Coming, George?'

'Well, I don't think . . .' He held up his whisky. 'Might as well finish this and then Beattie and me'll have to be getting back.'

The shadows were drawing in as the man and woman left the house and went round to the garage door. In the garden trees and flowers took on a ghostly look. Stephen opened the door and flung it wide. The garage looked oddly empty without Emily's car. There was Stephen's bicycle leaning against the wall, and a number of gardening tools.

'There's generally a spare can of petrol,' Stephen amplified, 'but Emily's taken that. It's only for emergencies, of course, but we're old-fashioned here. No garage open on a Sunday this side of Huntmere.'

Beattie, however, wasn't interested in petrol cans; she was staring at an enormous spade that leaned against the wall, clogged with damp earth.

'What on earth do you use that for?'

'Digging, of course.'

'That's no garden spade. It's more the kind of thing a sexton would have.'

'Well, I bought it at a sale. It was going cheap. Too big for most men, I dare say, but I like the feeling of heaving up a lot of earth at a time. There's this smaller one, because I used to fancy Emily might like to give me a hand at week-ends, but somehow she never took to it.'

'You've been digging quite recently,' Beattie accused him.

'That's right. I made an asparagus bed down beyond the orchard. That's one of the reasons I wanted this house, plenty of ground, and you never know when you can't do with a bit more. I did mean to make a real kitchen-garden there, but, well, it didn't prove practicable, me being away so much. And then, as I was telling Inspector Marston, Emily never really cared much about flowers. I'll have to buy you an aspidistra, I used to tell her, but I never did. Even ferns need a bit of care.'

'When were you digging?' demanded Beattie.

'Why, I've been at it most of the day.'

'And where? In the kitchen-garden?'

'I pruned the bushes. Show you if you like.'

But his voice was suddenly so strange and hostile that Beattie said she was like Emily, not all that mad on gardens and it was getting cold and she and George ought to be on their way.

In the dining-room George gulped down his whisky so hurriedly that he spilt a little on his coat. Looking round for something to mop up the spill—he could use his handkerchief, of course, but if he pulled it out later in the car Beattie would probably swoon—he saw a sheet of blotting paper on the desk. Just the job, thought George, picking it up. And then he forgot about the mark on his coat and stood goggle-eyed, staring at the small black hand-writing.

'My own darling,' he read. 'It won't be long now, the arrangements are made . . .'

The last words were faintly smudged as Stephen dashed the blotting paper down over the incriminating page.

George put the paper back, left the remainder of the whisky untasted and went into the hall just as Stephen and Beattie appeared from the garden.

'Thought you were burying yourselves there,' he said. 'Come on, you know how I hate to drive in the dark.'

He snatched up the little fur jacket and practically pushed her into it.

'Finish the other half of your whisky, George,' Stephen offered, but he said no, they had to be getting along.

'What was all that in aid of?' Beattie demanded, as the car turned into the main road. 'First time I've heard anything about you not liking driving in the dark.'

'I wanted to get out of the place. We don't want to find ourselves accessories.'

'Accessories to what?' asked Beattie.

'I don't know, but there's something wrong there. You felt it the same as I did. Beattie, there's another woman.'

And he told her about the letter.

'What did he say?' screamed Beattie, and George observed sourly it was a good thing it was a car he was driving and not a horse, give an animal forty fits to hear a female bawl like that.

'He knows Em's not coming back, that stuck out a mile. And that talk about taking up a new district. And a new Mrs. Tate, if you ask me. Beattie, I'm going to the police. You and I are going to be in the clear, whoever else isn't. What was that name he mentioned? Marsham?'

'Marston.'

'Right. We'll ask for this Inspector Marston and give him the facts and leave it to him to take any action he thinks appropriate.'

Marston heard this self-opinionated fussy little man without comment until he'd reached the end of his story. It all added up pretty well to him, he knew George wasn't the first to voice the belief that something fishy was going on at The Spinney.

'She wouldn't leave the shop without a word,' Beattie insisted. 'I know my sister. And not even telling her lawyer.'

'She may be in touch with her bankers,' said Marston, slowly.

But he remembered Spence saying, 'Must have fallen off a cliff or something not to have done anything about the takings.'

'Well, I'm reporting her as missing,' said George in dogged tones. 'If she's O.K. she's only got herself to thank making such a mystery.'

'It could be loss of memory,' Marston reminded them. He'd had his suspicions of Stephen, but he didn't want to be told his job by George Baynes.

'How about the car then?'

'You can suffer from loss of memory and still be able to drive a car,' Marston said.

But he knew he must take steps now, and if the missing woman and her husband were inconvenienced, well, they'd only got themselves to thank.

When Stephen saw Marston push open the gate of The Spinney late that evening he guessed what had happened. Beattie had made old George stop at the sign of the Blue Lamp and in about thirty seconds he was going to be treated to her version of the situation.

When he was officially told that his wife had been reported as a missing person, he exclaimed, 'What concern is it of George Baynes? My wife's perfectly capable of making her own decisions.' To which Marston replied in a grim voice, 'It's not surprising Mrs. Baynes should be anxious. After all, Emily is her sister.'

'If Emily wants Beattie to know where she is she'll write,' persisted Stephen doggedly.

But, of course, that got him nowhere. Marston said the matter would be treated in the routine way and had Stephen thought of anything he'd like to add to his previous statement. Stephen, obviously intending to be difficult, said he wasn't aware he'd made a statement, their previous conversation had been on an informal basis and he hadn't referred to the inspector by his official title. In any case, he had nothing to add. And as her husband, he chose to respect Emily's wish for privacy.

Marston remained unmoved. 'I'd like a few more details just the same, Mr. Tate. Would you know what your wife was wearing the day she disappeared?'

'As I didn't see her, the answer naturally is No.'

'If you were to look through her wardrobe you might be able to tell us what is missing,' Marston urged.

'She usually wore a sort of brown get-up,' said Stephen, hazily. 'But that doesn't mean she had no other coloured clothes.' He led the way upstairs. 'I've thought sometimes, if she'd been a bird, she'd have been a partridge. You know about them, Inspector? They can sink down into their surroundings so you could almost put your foot on them without seeing them. We humans think we're clever but Nature has always got there before us. Camouflage, you know.'

He led the way into Emily's room and indicated the big old-fashioned wardrobe with its glass panel, the high chest of drawers, the single hook behind the door.

'It all yours, Inspector. So far as I know, she didn't keep anything locked up.'

In the wardrobe a few drab garments were neatly arrayed on a rail. Dust and ashes, thought the inspector. Aloud he asked, 'Did she have a grey suit that you recall?'

'If she had she didn't wear it when I was at home. Why not ask young Spence? He looks the sort of fellow who'd notice a woman's clothes.'

There was no need to add that he himself was the kind of husband who'd hardly notice if his wife went out wearing nothing but woad.

'Yes, well, I was thinking about that button we found. You remember? Grey.'

'Oh, yes. So that's why you asked about the grey suit. Still, if we found it in the hall she'd be wearing the suit, wouldn't she?'

'If she was wearing a grey suit. But, of course, she might have had a visitor.'

'I suppose it's possible. I can't help you there, though.'

'If you could let me have the button, Mr. Tate . . .'

But Stephen said he couldn't say where it was now, he might have thrown it out, the inspector was free to hunt anywhere he liked. But Marston said quite pleasantly he didn't suppose he'd find it. He hadn't an atom of doubt that Stephen had contrived to return it to its original owner, unless he'd chucked it away.

But most likely it was at this instant securely fastened to the coat of 'My own darling.' He didn't press his man any further, he knew he could lay hands on Lily any time he wanted. Stephen might be tough, but he wouldn't be tough enough to stay away from the girl and there was no sense dragging her in before they had to. Shouldn't be hard to find out if she'd been in Little Wyvern that afternoon, but at the moment Stephen himself was the prime suspect.

'What was she wearing?' repeated young Spence. 'Why, her brown, of course. Had she got anything else? To tell you the truth, I thought she must have been born in it.'

'Didn't have silver buttons, I suppose?'

'Are you kidding? If she had anything silver it would have gone straight into the till to be transferred later to the bank. She might be a good business woman, though I have my doubts' (her refusal to take over the adjacent shop still rankled), 'but the only ornament she had any use for was a meek and quiet spirit, and she could even do without that.'

He repeated what he'd already told Marston on the fatal Thursday evening.

'I went round after I'd closed the shop soon after one, say one-thirty. I could hear the wireless going, two women's voices, jig, jig, jig, but though I rang two or three times she wouldn't answer. I thought she might be in the kitchen so I went round to the side and there was her car. But my luck wasn't in, and at that stage I didn't feel like breaking down the door.'

'What made you go?'

'I told you—I had the wigwag from a friend of mine in the house agent's, a dear girl if I hadn't met Harry first, that someone had made an offer for the shop, and if we wanted to get in on the ground floor there was no time to lose.'

'I thought she'd refused to entertain the idea.'

'I had a fresh proposal to make. Harry and I would pay the rent of the new place, sort of partnership, see. The details could be drawn up by her legal adviser, though it 'ud be a sharp chap who could put anything over on Mrs. T. No risk to her or not much, and the chance to cash in in a big way in, say, five years' time. Mind you, I think she probably knew who it was, peeped through the curtains—by the way, what do you suppose she had to hide? Those curtains wouldn't disgrace a black-out—and didn't mean to be hustled.'

'I've seen Armstrong,' Marston told him. Armstrong was the house agent. 'He says you went along that afternoon and left a note, giving the firm impression that she was going to make an offer for the premises.'

'Well.' All his facial powers came into play, he shrugged, he spread his hands. 'I wanted to jolly the old fellow along, and I felt I probably could talk her round. Anyway I got a stay of twenty-four hours. Inspector, do drop the Ku Kux Klan attitude and tell me what's cooking?'

Marston said woodenly that Mrs. Tate's family were afraid she might have lost her memory. Young Spence derided.

'If she lost a threepenny bit she'd put the woman in the Bible story to shame, you know, the one that lost the piece of silver. And she wouldn't go leaving her memory lying about, you take my word.'

Marston let that go. 'Have you got a note of the figures you paid in last week?' he said.

Spence produced the bank's receipt. Then he said, 'There's some funny business going on, Inspector,' and now suddenly he was dead serious.

'Yes?'

'You know I said she never confides in me, well, no reason why she should, I'm not her partner—yet. But—take a look at this.'

He opened the paying-in book. 'That's last week's total. Pretty average. We'll be a bit up for a week or two because people seem to think it's worth buying something that keeps anyway and that you're bound to want sooner or later in the hopes of picking up a bit of dirt. But look back . . .' He turned several sheets one by one. 'I'll swear that doesn't represent the week's takings. Ergo, she wasn't paying it all in. Well, we know she's dead keen on paying cash on the nail, but even so, it's not as if it were just one week. Right back for three months and more, and the business hasn't fallen off, that I do assure you. See what I'm getting at?'

'I passed my equivalent of the eleven-plus quite a while ago,' the inspector assured him. 'You mean, Mrs. Tate hasn't been paying in the whole of the takings.'

'Of course she could have her reasons,' young Spence admitted, handsomely. 'Found a cache of notes anywhere in The Spinney? Or haven't you started taking up the floor-boards yet?'

'You're wasted in your present job,' said Marston smoothly, but Spence shook his head.

'None of that, Inspector. I'm not tall enough to be a policeman. Well, of course, I can see that's what you have in mind. Look, if there's nothing more I can tell you, could I get back to the shop? Bert's probably started giving things away by this time.'

Walking away from the chemist's shop Marston decided there were two explanations that might be considered in regard to the noticeable fall in moneys paid in by Emily during the past three months or so. She might have been putting aside a certain amount of cash each week because she knew she was planning her own disappearance, and didn't want to have to apply to the bank for funds, or she might have been keeping the money to pay off a secret debt. He had had too much experience of police work to dismiss the most unlikely possibilities of blackmail; her position would give her special temptations, she might have fallen foul of her associates and she couldn't afford to court publicity. But surely even someone as single-minded as a woman would have realised that her unexplained disappearance would bring the authorities on to the scene and precipitate the very limelight she was anxious to avoid? He went to the bank at Chelston and learned that during the first two months of the year Emily had drawn sums of £100 in notes; during the next three months the takings she had paid in had decreased by approximately the same amount. The inference seemed obvious. She hadn't confided in her husband or, so far as he could discover, in anyone else.

A police officer went to 24 Curtonbridge Street, which

proved to be the usual small newsagent-cum-confectioner. A notice in the window said the telephone could be used and letters could be left there. The woman behind the counter was a Mrs. Rodding, a plumpish middle-aged party with swags of fair hair turning grey. She looked obligingly through some letters awaiting collection but there was nothing for A. M. She said she didn't recall the initials, but added honestly that she didn't pay much attention to such envelopes in any case.

'Half the time they're kids who don't want their families to know they're writing,' she said. 'Spinsters living at home and sending for beauty treatments. I wonder sometimes why they don't use the post office. Cheaper, you'd think.'

'You're a stranger here,' suggested the officer pleasantly, and she said, Well, yes, she was. She'd taken the place over from Mr. Samuelson a few months back, and he told her it was a little gold mine. 'But he was stringing me along, unless he had a different kind of clientele from mine. You can't charge more than fourpence for a telephone call and the letters don't bring in such a lot. There's the display case in the front, of course.' She indicated a frame full of small cards advertising private wants. Daily Women, three shillings an hour. Things for sale. Clothes, baby-pens, furniture. Sixpence a week she charged for those and not many stayed up more than the fortnight. She had her real trade, of course, and there was the usual profit there, but it was a bare living, taken one way and another. 'In my husband's time I had a car and I miss that,' she said. 'But what I take wouldn't keep a three-wheeler going.'

The police had had some difficulty in finding a photograph of Emily. Stephen said they'd never had any taken since they married, and the wedding had been very quiet and no photographers invited. The best authority could do was blow up a bit of a snapshot Beattie had provided, and the result wasn't startlingly helpful. All the same, the policeman produced it.

Mrs. Rodding shook her head. 'I don't know it, but that doesn't mean she didn't come here. She might have worn a veil or a hat over her face, like some of them do. . . .'

'Why?' interrupted the policeman.

Mrs. Rodding looked at him thoughtfully. 'Well, there's the few who wouldn't use the post office come what may. I mean, I did get your point, in a small place people recognise you and if you're seen asking at the post office for a letter some might start adding two and two, and it isn't everyone that's so good at arithmetic. But you can always tell the ones whose letters are important. In the first place, they never ask outright if there's a letter. They'll want cigarettes or a bar of chocolate or a paper of some sort, and if anyone else comes in they won't say a word but dodge back afterwards. Then when they've paid they'll say as if it's just occurred to them, "Was there a letter, by the way?" and you can tell by the way they take it. . . . Still, it's no business of mine. Who's that meant to be?' She indicated the photograph.

The policeman told her.

'That's the one who's missing, isn't it? Oh yes, you hear all the talk. Any reason to suppose she hasn't gone of her own free-will?'

'People who want to disappear 'ud do better to take us into their confidence,' said the policeman.

'Perhaps she has her reasons. Well, if anything should come for A. M. I'll let you know, naturally.'

A woman came into the shop, saw the policeman, gave a faint start and then a smile and asked for a packet of Woodbines. She paid and went out of the shop. The policeman looked after her. He hadn't any doubt she was one of those who used the accommodation address for some serious purpose, a skinny little thing who'd shaken hands with youth a long time ago. Talk about the mysterious universe, he thought. One huge crossword puzzle with half the clues not making sense anyway.

In the meantime Emily had been seen all over the country; she surfaced in half a dozen places on the same day. 'Good thing for her we've abolished capital punishment for witchcraft,' said Marston. 'Anyone who can be in York, Llanelly and Brighton at the same time ought to be Prime Minister.'

They got in touch with Mr. Negus, but he couldn't help either.

He said it was his father who made the joint wills for the Tates when they married, each leaving whatever they had to the other. About two years before Emily had asked for her will, saying she wanted to amend it, and that was all they'd heard.

'My father retired about that time,' agreed Thomas Negus. 'I took over most of the jobs, and whether a letter we wrote her in another connection annoyed her or whether she took a fancy to some other lawyer I couldn't say.'

All he could say was he didn't know anything about a new will.

Beattie was jumping around like a flea in a gale of wind. 'If there isn't another will then her money goes to her next-of-kin,' she said. 'That would be me.'

'Hold your horses,' begged George. 'For all we know Emily's lying up somewhere laughing her head off.'

He'd even begun to think the impossible had happened and she'd gone off, à la Camille Holland. In which case, sooner or later, they'd get news. It wasn't as though she and Stephen had ever been Romeo and Juliet, and she'd known about this girl. And then it struck him as odd that the girl so far hadn't had much of a show. He supposed the police hadn't tracked her down and old Stephen was keeping his big mouth shut. One way and another, there was a lot of missing things in this case— Emily, the car, the girl, the will. He had a little bet with himself which of them would turn up first.

And in point of fact, it was the car.

CHAPTER V

I T was found quite by chance by a pair of hikers during the Whitsun week-end. Where does a wise man hide a leaf? inquired G. K. Chesterton. And the answer, of course, is in the forest. And so it was with the car.

During the latter part of the war a German bomber, being smartly chased back across the Channel, had dumped his load in the woods beyond Chelston in the direction of Huntmere, creating an area of devastation that an enterprising public had later used as a graveyard for the kind of refuse for which there is no market but that local Councils can't be expected to remove. It began with old saucepans, basins, cracked crockery, discarded as things eased and it was possible to replace them; then followed the ancient stoves, rusted car parts, rotten tyres, until eventually whole chassis were deposited there, to rot and rust, be occasionally employed by birds for nesting purposes, until the cats that had run wild in the war came sneaking up and stalking the enterprising parents. Anything worth half-a-crown had been looted long ago, and even the youth of the neighbourhood had abandoned the place as an entertainment centre. Every now and again questions were asked at local Council meetings, but no one had a workable alternative to propose and it was unsightly rather than unhygienic.

In the sort of weather the countryside was enduring that season even the lovers shunned the spot, and the youthful hikers, who were spending the inclement holiday at a nearby hostel only stumbled on it by accident.

Thanks to the furious onset of the rain they had decided to attempt a short cut which, as so often happens, proved the longest way home. But at least the police should have been grateful to them. The girl looked about her.

'You need a death certificate before you can be buried,' she suggested. 'Or were you thinking we might shelter in one of these ruins? They'd probably break in half if you put a foot on the running-board.'

Her companion frowned. He had a narrow clever face above a black turtle-necked sweater.

'There's something rum here,' he said, looking at the sea of rusted and battered chassis, tyreless wheels, old car seats, ripped up and discarded. 'Look at those.' He indicated the tyres of a small hacked-about looking car. 'Why hasn't anyone pinched them?'

'I suppose because they aren't any good,' returned the girl, impatiently.

'That's were you're wrong. They're not even worn smooth. There's no rust or practically none, and—look here, Ava—most of the damage is deliberate. The car seats have been hacked with a knife or scissors, they're not worn out, they're mutilated. And the paint-work—it looks to me as though someone's used a hatchet on this job.'

As he stooped above it the thunder suddenly rolled and the lightning flashed.

'You don't want to be in the middle of a sea of metal with the lightning blazing,' said the girl, rather crossly. But he was absorbed.

'The upholstery's been slashed about, it hasn't worn out, the car's been abandoned.' He looked round with a practised eye. 'We're standing in a slight hollow. Someone sent this car ricocheting down from above, and it must have made an almighty clangour when it struck this hulk.' He laid his hand on something so dilapidated it was hard to believe it had ever been serviceable. 'Someone wanted to smash it.'

'Someone drunk?'

'If he'd been drunk he'd probably have smashed himself with the car.' He looked round. 'No number-plates. Oh well, I suppose there's always a market for them.' Then he stopped. 'Perhaps that's the answer, perhaps it's a stolen car. I wonder if we should tell the police.'

All this time they were getting steadily wetter. It was the girl who said, 'Wasn't there some talk at that hostel last night about someone missing? Some woman . . . Landladies had been alerted.'

'Wanted by the police?' he inquired, vaguely.

'I suppose so. There was something about a car. All the same, I don't see why this should be it.'

He walked round and looked through the shattered windows. 'No body,' he announced, 'and, so far as one can see, no blood.' He tried one of the doors. 'Locked. That doesn't make sense—or does it?' He put his hand on the boot. 'That's locked too. You don't suppose . . . ?'

'No, she couldn't. Not unless she's a dwarf.'

'Or one of your friends has been called in to help.' She was a medical student and already the first nausea brought about by the dissection room had passed.

The boy looked round as if he expected to see a field-telephone attached to a tree. 'We're quite near the river,' he said. 'If we cut down there we're not more than ten minutes from the bridge.' He looked about him. 'It's like a bit of no-man's land, no houses, no anything. You could probably ditch half a dozen corpses without attracting any attention except from the crows. And the weir's not far off. . . .' He was working it all out method-ically. 'What else did you hear about this woman?'

'She came from Little Wyvern.'

'That's the other side of the Pyne. Come on. We may be stick-ing our necks out, but if that car has no owner she's worth sal-vaging.' He was an engineer himself. 'Can't have been there very long or someone would have spotted it.'

The weather of recent weeks had been shocking, no temptation to anyone to trudge through the woods to this lonely place.

'If we don't get a move on we shall drown,' suggested Ava, im-patiently. 'Then we shall make the headlines all right. Two drown at Mystery Mile or whatever the place is called.'

They came plunging down through the mud and the undergrowth till they reached the bridge; this was so sopping there was practically no traffic, but a car could cross all right, though heavy lorries were forbidden. The boy, whose imagination was the keener, had a picture in his mind of a mysterious hooded figure driving the little car on some dark night, say, into the woods, having first relieved it of its burden. The river current swirled dangerously here, a body would be swept downstream, be caught into the overhanging roots or rushed over the weir, and after that it was anybody's guess where it might land. They tramped the two miles to the police station, meeting no one; the rain had set in in a steady downpour and sensible people were having an early cup of tea and turning on the television or the wireless. The picture-houses would do well to-day. At the station they were allowed to dry off by the fire when they'd told their story, and given cups of tea. It seemed more than probable that this was Emily's car, and the first thing to do was to open the boot and see what was inside. Just her bag most likely, said the girl, but her companion scowled again.

'Not much sense removing the number plates and giving her a bashing if he was going to leave her clothes on board,' he said. 'Why not chuck them into the river, too? A couple of heavy stones and drop it off the middle of the bridge, wouldn't surface till Kingdom Come. How deep's the river there, officer?'

They forced the lock of the car and of the boot, but there was no luggage, no handbag, and, as the boy had surmised, no stains of blood. But when they came to give her a good going-over they found something so small it would be easy to overlook it, something all the same that might incriminate a man.

They went round to The Spinney to talk to Stephen and here they met their first obstruction, for Stephen wasn't there.

CHAPTER VI

STEPHEN was spending the holiday break at Lily's cottage. For appearance's sake he had booked a room at a hotel a mile or so distant, but it was with his love that he spent all his waking hours. In this part of the world, too, the weather was atrocious, but neither paid any heed to the pelting rain and the black skies. Sitting by the fire in the old-fashioned grandfather chair with its ears to keep off the draughts, Stephen had the feeling that his previous life was shut away by some barrier, like a gate that had been locked and the key lost, so that he couldn't get back even if he wanted to. He said as much to his companion.

Lily shivered.

'Goose walking over my grave,' she explained. 'It makes me think of a story I once read, about a man who suddenly found the road in front of him had turned into a blind alley, and when he turned back the road he'd taken had disappeared, closed up behind him, made him a prisoner.'

'You can't relive the past,' Stephen pointed out. In all his life he had never known such a sense of security as now possessed him, which of itself showed he was besotted with love not to perceive the perils that encompassed him on every side. Since his mother's death twenty years earlier he had never had anyone utterly dependent upon him. Not, that is, as Lily was dependent now. Here at last was a creature leaning against him for support, drawing her whole life from the fact of his existence. He was savouring the delights of this enchanted yet forbidden love when the bell of the cottage rang peremptorily.

'Who can that be on Bank Holiday Monday?' he wondered.

'Someone wanting to use a telephone, I expect. I'll go.' Her voice was full of peace.

'But you haven't got a telephone.'

'They never seem to notice. Or perhaps they've lost their way. Or want water for their radiator.'

'Let them catch it in their own hats,' said Stephen unsympathetically.

'It might even be an accident.'

Even as she turned to the door as the bell rang for the second time she paused, stooping to kiss him like a wife, like a wife . . . He heard the door open and a man's voice, and then Lily answering. And footsteps. Someone was coming in. Instantly apprehensive he was on his feet.

'It's someone for you, Stephen.'

'On Bank Holiday?' he asked stupidly. It was inconceivable he could have forgotten about Emily even for five minutes.

They told him about the car.

'What makes them think it's hers?'

'I don't doubt they'll tell you at Chelston,' said the man.

He shook a big bewildered head. 'You mean, you expect me to come along now?' But, of course, he knew that was what they meant.

He wasn't even permitted five minutes alone with Lily; he wondered how they'd tracked him down, not realising that, as the husband of the missing woman, they'd been on his trail almost from the first. They went with him to his hotel, a second policeman driving his car. 'Crouch isn't going to like this,' he said mechanically. As they drove off he turned to watch Lily standing by the door, staring out at the wild streaming night, her hair blown all ways by the sodden wind. He thought that memory would stay with him all his life long.

They didn't take him along to see the car that night. A man from the All Seasons garage, who'd serviced Emily's car, identified it by means of a special kind of mat she'd put in it and by the covers on the seats which they had supplied. Instead Stephen found himself confronted by Marston, who opened his hand to show him what they'd found in the abandoned car.

'Do you recognise that ear-ring, Mr. Tate?'

He stared at it mistrustfully. He knew it, of course. It always seemed strange to him that Emily, so puritanical in her dress, invariably wore the ear-rings that had belonged to her mother, each a pearl set in a diamond circle. True, the diamonds were small, but the pearl was the genuine article and he'd never thought they looked right with her drab tweeds and high-buttoning silk blouses.

'Where did you find that?' he inquired.

'In the car.'

'I suppose it could have slipped while she was driving.'

'Oh, we don't think she was driving,' said Marston. 'I mean, she'd hardly be driving from the back seat.'

'Is that where you found it?'

'Crammed down among the cushions.'

To his own horror Stephen burst into a rusty sort of laugh. 'You're not trying to tell me that Emily was necking in the back of her car? Oh come, Inspector . . .'

'You know what I'm telling you, Mr. Tate.'

'You mean, she was in the back seat? It doesn't sound like Emily. She hated being a passenger, even when we went out in my car, which didn't happen often, she could hardly bear to let me drive. She had the feeling that anything she did she did better than anyone else.'

'No,' agreed Marston, 'it doesn't sound like Emily. It doesn't sound like Emily to have a passenger at all, and if she had she'd still be sitting in the front, wouldn't she? Well, wouldn't she?' His voice suddenly became unbelievably threatening. 'And if she'd been going off for a few days she'd have had her luggage in the car, and there's no luggage there now.' He leaned so close now that his face almost touched Stephen's. 'The game's up,' he said, 'quit stalling. We've been on this job long enough. Where is she?'

Stephen tried to pull back. 'I've told you, I don't know.'

'I said to stop that. We've got the ear-ring, we've got the car. Emily thought a lot of that car. She'd never have savaged it the way it's been savaged and not just by weather. So, come on, Mr. Tate—*where is she?*'

'Isn't it your job to find her?'

'Oh, we'll do that all right. And since we're on the subject, where's the other half of that letter, the half you didn't show us?'

'I've told you, that's all there was. If there was another half Emily destroyed it.'

'Young Spence says he heard voices when he came round at lunch-time; was one of them yours?'

'I wasn't there at lunch-time. I went back to my hotel and made up my accounts and came down in the afternoon.'

'You could prove that?'

'I suppose so. I had a sandwich and a beer in the bar. Someone might remember.'

'You're known at that hotel?'

'Actually I hadn't used it before.'

'What time did you check out?'

'I took my luggage when I left in the morning.'

'What time did you reach Chelston? You came by train?'

'I told you I did.'

'You've been living in the neighbourhood for more than twelve years. Someone would recognise you.'

'It was Market Day in Chelston. You wouldn't recognise your own mother in that crush.'

'You think of everything, don't you, Mr. Tate?'

'I can't think where Emily is, if that's what you're driving at.'

'And you can't think of any reason why she should wreck her own car and stay hidden with a nation-wide search going on for her?'

'I can't, and that's a fact. But then there's a great deal about Emily I don't know, even if she is my wife. There was Rouse, remember.'

'Rouse? How does he come into this?'

'He wanted to give the impression he was dead, and he burned a strange man in his car in the hope that the corpse would be taken for his.'

'Well, we didn't find any body in Emily's car. And can you suggest a single reason why she should want to disappear?'

'I've just told you, I don't know half the things about Emily there were to be known. In a way, she's been a stranger to me all through our married life. We rubbed along like a good many couples, but that's about the size of it.'

'And you're asking us to believe she was in some trouble and planned this elaborate disappearance?'

'I'm asking you to consider the possibility.'

'She wasn't a fool, she'd know she couldn't get away with it.'

'Would she? You should look at your records. Think of the chaps who've escaped from Her Majesty's prisons and been at large for months with the whole country on the *qui vive*. Remember when Neville Heath was wanted and the whole police force had his picture, but he got away with a second murder before he was caught. And we don't know, we simply don't know, how many people there may be at this moment living quietly under assumed names and no one suspects their real identity. There's this money she's been drawing or withholding for months, that would keep her going for quite a while. . . .'

'Now come, Mr. Tate, you know you don't believe that. How about the shop?'

'Well, then, why don't you get after A. M.?' demanded the harassed husband. 'Wouldn't that be the best way?'

'Oh, yes,' agreed Marston. 'A. M. Too bad you can't help us there. I suppose A. M. wouldn't have a twin sister called Mrs. Harris.'

Stephen put his face in his hands. Marston didn't give him any respite; it doesn't do the police any good when a suspect manages to swallow something lethal in the course of a criminal investigation.

'Now,' Marston continued, 'there's the matter of Miss Vane.'

'You can leave her out of it,' Stephen snapped.

'Now you know that's absurd. The young lady was there on the day Emily vanished.'

'Who says so?'

'You're not forgetting the button?'

'You've yet to prove it's hers.'

'She was wearing a grey suit with silver buttons when the

officer called this afternoon. It's true he couldn't identify them, but I doubt if I'd be far wrong if I said I'd already handled one of them. Now, Mr. Tate, might it be that when you came back that Thursday you found Emily dead at The Spinney?'

'You should be writing for television,' said Stephen savagely. 'I've told you already I didn't see my wife alive or dead, I have had no communication from her and I have no more notion at the moment than you yourself where she may be.'

'If you had found the body and concealed it . . .'

Stephen interrupted. 'If I'd found a body I'd have rung you right away. Trying to conceal corpses is a mug's game.'

'It depends on circumstances,' said Marston slowly, and Stephen knew he was thinking of the silver button.

'I hadn't seen the button,' he pointed out rashly. 'I didn't know . . .'

'That Miss Vane had been there? But you know now? Oh well,' as Stephen maintained a mulish silence, 'we shall have her evidence.'

Stephen lumbered to his feet. 'You've no right to question her, she's innocent, she doesn't understand about tricks and traps, she has a right to have a lawyer present. . . .'

'She'll be warned of her rights, and if she hasn't anything to conceal . . .'

'Of course she has something to conceal. Once she lets your chaps know she was there that day she'll be harried and bullied. . . .'

'You've no call to say that, Mr. Tate.'

But Stephen was past wisdom and reason alike. 'If she could have told you anything she'd have come forward already. I note you didn't suggest bringing her down with me.'

'She doesn't live here.'

He looked about him wildly. 'Where's a telephone? No, that's no use, she hasn't got one.'

For an instant Marston thought there might be actual physical violence. He had never seen his companion so perturbed. He was so crazy that he now made a suggestion no man in his right senses would expect the police to consider.

'You haven't thought this may be a deliberate thing on Emily's part? Suppose she had found out about me and Lily—don't ask me how, Emily had her own way of doing things—and this is her revenge?'

'A rather elaborate one, wouldn't you suggest?'

'You didn't know Emily even as well as I did. She had a spiteful streak, I learned that soon after I was married. Even with her own father, and you'd have said they'd be devoted enough, same interests and living together all those years—she was his housekeeper from the time she was sixteen and I know she was on tenterhooks for some time in case he married again. But even there I've known her watch him with something like hate—yes, I mean it, Inspector. She had to be first, and she never liked him talking to me as much as he did, asking my advice. And that's why she wouldn't share the shop with me after he'd gone. She had to be first. Even though her feeling for me wasn't what you might look for in a wife . . .'

'If Emily had wanted to get even with you she wouldn't have chosen this way,' Marston insisted.

'All right then, but why don't you set your chaps to tracking down someone who saw her leave the place that Thursday? The car couldn't have driven itself there alone in broad daylight.'

'Who says it was broad daylight? By the way, there's another point you might clear up. You were sitting in your kitchen in the small hours of Friday morning. We've got a witness to that effect.'

'I never heard there was a law to stop a man sitting in his own kitchen at any hour of the day or night.'

'Still! One o'clock in the morning. You have a lounge. . . .'

'No one ever lounged at The Spinney. Emily wouldn't have stood for it. In any case, I preferred the kitchen. It seemed more—more homely. The rest of the house, with Emily gone, had a sort of haunted feeling. She had—has—a lot of character, for all she's only a little bit of a thing. I didn't feel like sleep, so I thought I'd fill in some time mending my bike.'

'Mending your bike?'

'Yes. I told you I was going over to Radford next day. I hadn't got my car and public transport's no help, so I have a bicycle. I remembered there was a puncture, so I went along to the garage to mend it. That was how I found I'd lost the key and went down to the river-bank to find it. You remember?'

'I remember. What made you lock the garage and take the key with you?'

'I had my bike there; it's a pretty good one with various fitments. Not altogether up to date, perhaps, but it suits me. And seeing there'd be no one on the premises . . . All right, Inspector, where do we go from here?'

'Any objection if we go to The Spinney?' inquired Marston.

Stephen grinned savagely. 'Have I any choice? Aren't you the boss?'

'I haven't got a search warrant,' Marston confessed. 'I can apply for one to the Magistrates' Court as soon as it sits again. Until then I've no right to walk in and search your house. I'd like you to know where you stand.'

'And if I refuse I suppose that lends colour to your imagination. Oh, come up. We may as well get it over with.'

So they got into a police car and went over to the desolate house. The general impression was of a scene of despair. The storm had brought down branches, laid wild the flower-beds, even damaged the hardy monkey-puzzler. Stephen stood at the window staring out; the bald light laid an illumination over the dishevelled beds.

'They've had it bad here,' he said, almost conversationally. 'These were planted as deep as a grave.'

One of the policemen gave a start; no one answered. Stephen smiled wryly.

'Carry on, gentlemen,' he suggested. 'Do you want a guide or do I wait here while you . . . ?'

But of course they weren't going to leave him alone. He preceded them through the house, flinging open doors. 'My room, my wife's room, spare-room, second spare-room—we call this one the Mouse-trap, belonged to a slavey in the Miss Lewises' day, I suppose, or a visiting dwarf, I wouldn't know. This is a box-room—if you were thinking my wife might be here . . .' Furiously he flung open a cupboard door and for an instant the youngest of the policemen anticipated a grotesque body falling out, stiff as Mrs. Noah, but nothing of the sort happened. The shelves were full of the sort of old junk all households collect over the years. There was a curtain hanging in one corner, but there was nothing behind that but a few hooks, with an ancient raglan coat suspending from one of them.

Stephen stamped heavily on the floorboards.

'Beautiful work,' he commented. 'The old ladies had the best of everything. D'you know, we've never even had a leak in the roof. That's one of the reasons I wanted the house, that and the garden, of course.'

Insensibly one of the policemen glanced through the grey square of window. (Curtains in a box-room? Emily had said. What nonsense!)

The police found nothing to help them in their solution of the mystery, though they searched everywhere, tested walls and floors. There was no trace of Emily, no blood—but, of course, there didn't have to be blood—and Mrs. Rorke had been at her mischievous best, setting the place to rights and destroying any clues a criminal (a murderer?) might have left. Not that she wouldn't have reported anything untoward that caught her malicious eye. Stephen opened the cocktail cabinet and poured himself a shot of whisky. The policeman who'd been left to guard him watched him with eyes like a hawk to make certain he didn't slip himself a Mickey Finn. Marston remembered young Spence saying, 'Wouldn't surprise me if Mr. Emily Purdy did slip her a Mickey Finn.' Mr. Emily Purdy. Was that the explanation? Had she made it clear, too clear for her own good, that she was the boss? No one knew much about their private affairs, they were as cagey as the Bank of England, but no doubt she had considered the grey mare to be the better horse. Five-and-twenty years as a policeman had warned Marston that jealousy is a machine-gun in the hand of a husband or wife, she might have driven him beyond control. But if she had she was back in the saddle now—he smiled wryly at the realisation of his mixed metaphors. Though if she was dead, as at bottom he suspected she was, it wouldn't do her much good.

Stephen carried his whisky over to the fire-place, where the electric fire blazed a consoling red.

'Where the body is there shall the vultures be gathered together,' he remarked. 'Only, you haven't got a body yet, have you?'

Upstairs the men were working as if they'd been promised a bonus. Stephen heard doors being jerked open and drawers run in and out. They were so long about it he wondered aloud if they were peeling the paper off the walls.

'When I was a kid,' he said suddenly to his escort, a man called Hammond, 'my mother used to tell me stories. I remember one was about a farmer whose cows all disappeared and he told his boy to find them p.d.q. When the lad asked where he should look, the farmer said, "In all the likely places and in all the unlikely ones." When he came back from his rounds he found all his flowers uprooted and the boy was up on the roof among the chimney-stacks. "What the hell are you doing up there?" bawled the farmer. "You told me to look in all the likely places and in all the unlikely ones," the boy replied. "And I'm looking in the unlikely ones first." '

The policeman looked embarrassed.

'It was a good story, wasn't it?' Stephen persisted. 'Think yourself back into the skin of a kid of five. What a lark it would be to pull up the pansies and smash the tiles. Oh, well. Don't you want to get yourself some tea or something?'

But the man said that was all right, thank you, and silence came down again. Stephen tried to while away the time picturing to himself exactly what was going on upstairs; he wondered if you could bring a suit against the police for wilful damage; he thought how little the average citizen knows about his own rights; and he recalled Marston saying, 'Don't make any further statement without legal advice.' But I haven't got a lawyer, he discovered. Negus had looked over the lease for The Spinney and advised him about trivial matters on one or two occasions. But apart from that he had never needed a lawyer. It was Negus, too, who had drawn up his will, leaving Emily his sole beneficiary. It had occurred to him at the time that he could make another or add an appropriate codicil when the children came, but there had never been any children, so the matter had never arisen. After that he thought he must have dozed off for a few minutes, improbable though it seemed, but his time-clock had stopped and the one on the chimney-piece had no meaning. An eternity seemed to separate him from the man who had sat beside his pretty Lily's fire and felt the silken softness of her hair. He liked to think she wouldn't recognise the secretly shivering wretch waiting to learn what the next step would be. And he wondered what was happening to her. No way of finding out, since you could be sure they wouldn't let her telephone. He thanked his stars she couldn't drive a car, so surely they couldn't link her up with Emily's disappearance.

It seemed an age before the police were through; short of counting every lump of coal in the cellar and actually taking down the walls they'd made a pretty good job of it. They hadn't discounted the possibility of the body being under the floor but in most of the rooms it was obvious the boards hadn't been disturbed in years; there were flags in the kitchen covered with a cord carpet, but these were cemented down and there was no evidence that anyone had even attempted to disturb them. And there was no sign of a pick anywhere. There was no sign of Emily's handbag, either.

'It's news to me,' said Stephen, 'that you can try and hold a man for a crime that so far as you know hasn't been committed.'

'Well, the fact is, Mr. Tate, there's a lot we don't know. But we shall find out.'

'Till you've got a body,' Stephen began, but the inspector said, 'Don't forget George Camb. And Haigh, too, come to that.'

'There was the Camberwell Mystery where three people were hanged on account of a man who proved later not to be dead. Don't you forget that.'

His nerve was beginning to break. Marston watched him acutely. This was often the moment of truth.

'We won't,' he said in reply to Stephen's last remark.

But as though sudden wisdom had popped up to warn him Stephen shut up like a clam.

'I've nothing more to tell you,' he said. 'Dig the whole place over, I'm sure you intend to anyway, though, if I had killed my wife, I hope I'd have too much sense to put her in my own garden. Don't forget the lawn, of course. It's news to me anyone can dig up turf and leave no trace, but your chaps are such smart alecs. . . .'

They left the man called Hammond on duty at The Spinney.

'Does that mean I'm under arrest?'

'For what, Mr. Tate? You've just pointed out, no one can be arrested without evidence that a crime's been committed, and it wouldn't be the first time a lady had disappeared without leaving a message—it's called loss of memory sometimes. Perhaps Emily is suffering from that. Only we've got to act on any evidence we can find, and it doesn't seem likely she'd remember to remove the plates from her car and walk through all that mud to a hotel, and no one remember it.'

He hadn't expected to sleep, but he did, and next morning when he looked out of his windows, there they were digging away like moles.

'Getting a bit of free gardening,' said Stephen to Hammond, who brought him a cup of tea. 'I hope to goodness they know what they're about. By the way, I'm afraid the larder's a bit under-stocked.'

But Hammond said not to worry, they'd look after that.

'Am I allowed to go out?' he inquired.

'Why not?' asked Marston. 'You're not under arrest. Naturally we shouldn't expect you to leave the neighbourhood. But, unless you've got some particular reason, you might prefer to stay inside.'

He went away and Stephen mooched over to the window. The Spinney was an isolated house, and often you could stand and watch the empty road for as long as it amused you. But not to-day. Little Wyvern was having a free show. At any minute the police might find a body in the garden—they'd practically torn the house to pieces, but even in the disused cellar they'd discovered no signs of foul play. He glimpsed young Eastham, and abruptly rattled a curtain along the rod. Take the inspector's advice, he thought. Stay put. If anyone rings the bell let Hammond answer it.

Presently he telephoned Mr. Crouch. He pulled no punches in explaining his situation. 'My wife has disappeared and they have the original idea that the husband may be responsible. In the circumstances, the police prefer my company to my room.'

Mr. Crouch tcha-ed, tcha-ed! A shocking thing. Most painful. (And not good for the company, not good at all, his voice implied.) Better stay put for the moment, and he'd get Ferrers to carry on, and leave their implied new arrangement in the air till the police came down one side of the fence or the other.

'They should give you a medal,' suggested Stephen, gently. 'Co-operating with authority.' He heard Mr. Crouch gasp as he hung up the receiver.

As soon as Stephen had departed from the cottage on the Green, a second police car took Lily to the local station. Here she was cautioned and told she need answer no questions without legal advice. She said simply, 'I've nothing to hide. Not now.'

She repeated the story she had told Stephen.

'You knew we were inquiring for Mrs. Tate, why didn't you come forward?'

'Why should I? I couldn't tell you anything. She was alive at midday on Thursday. Well, you knew that. Mr. Spence had told you. She wasn't there when Mr. Tate arrived that evening. What happened after my departure and his coming I don't know.'

'You say you weren't allowed inside the house?'

'Just over the threshold. I didn't want to come any farther, she terrified me.'

'And you came straight back?'

'I walked to Chelston and caught the next train.'

'Did you see anyone you knew on the train?'

'No. But I wouldn't expect to.'

'And when you arrived back?'

'I came to my own house.'

'Again seeing no one?'

'Seeing no one.'

'So what it amounts to is you've no witness of your movements that day.'

'Only Mrs. Tate.'

'Did you ring up anyone on your return?'

'How could I? I don't have a line.'

'There's a box on the Green.'

'Oh, yes. But I didn't use it.'

'Did Mr. Tate know you were going to see his wife?'

'I didn't know myself till that morning.'

'And when did you tell him you'd been?'

'I didn't have to. He knew.'

'How was that?'

Lily said indifferently, 'I suppose she told him.'

'Didn't you know that according to him she was gone before he returned?'

'Oh, yes. Well, then, it must have been the button. A button got torn off my coat, and he found it and brought it back to me.'

'Torn off?'

'Mrs. Tate was furious. If there's been a murder you'd have expected it to be her.'

'Did Mr. Tate say anything about a murder?'

'Of course not. He thought she'd left him because of me.'

They plodded on with all the routine questions. Had she noticed anyone in the road, coming or going? What time was her train? Was it late, early, plumb on time? Had she noticed any of her fellow travellers. Did she have a car? Could she drive? In her own way she was as unhelpful as Stephen. She said: 'No. Three-fifteen. Five minutes behind time. No. No. No.'

Eventually they let her return to The Cottage, where loneliness greeted her like a host, and there was nothing to do but wait and think about her lover.

She longed to write to him but dared not. She couldn't telephone on the Green because she felt besieged in her little house.

The newspaper she called for each morning on her way to work remained accumulating in the shop; the milkman left milk and butter and eggs, the baker left bread; anything else was brought by a sympathetic neighbour, a lamb chop, a packet of bacon, vegetables. She let the things stay in the porch all day. She kept the front curtains drawn and sat at the back of the house. After nightfall she peeped cautiously out and if the coast seemed clear she opened the door a few inches and snatched in the supplies. Even this wasn't altogether safe; the three trees at the gate would be mysteriously multiplied into four and then she knew someone was watching. One enterprising pressman got into a house a little farther down on the opposite side and snapped her as she made her desperate survey. The postman knocked, he'd never brought so many letters before. They came all shapes and sizes and after a day or two she learned to destroy them unread. Once she was actually caught by an enterprising reporter.

'Have you a statement to make? Come, Miss Vane, you owe a duty to the public.'

'I owe nothing to anyone. Why can't you leave us alone?'

She put on the wireless to listen to the news. There was trouble all over the world, in Algeria, in the Congo, in New York; she didn't care. She listened, rigid as a dutch doll, to hear Stephen's name. One day she would know what happened to him. Mr. Davies even came to call but she wouldn't let him in. She trusted no one.

The odd thing was she never gave a thought to Emily; her heart beat Stephen, Stephen, Stephen. Sometimes in the silence she thought she could hear his beating Lily, Lily, Lily.

It was much the same at The Spinney, where the police went on hunting for a body that obstinately refused to surface. Stephen watched them from the window. He didn't go out. Food appeared on the table, he never asked how. Hammond seemed to have taken up residence there. One day Stephen asked him if he played chess; he didn't, but Emily had had a scrabble board and they sat for hours over that. Hammond, who was shaky on spelling, asked if he could have a replacement. Not a bit of it, said Marston. Free education's one of the blessings of the Welfare

State. Often he spelt his words wrong. Stephen never corrected him. Anyone can spell with the aid of a dictionary, he thought. It takes imagination to spell things wrong. Mrs. Rorke called one morning and was sent away with an outsize flea in her ear. Beattie drove over and had the door slammed in her face. She was interviewed by the Press and the result was featured. George was horrified. 'Stephen could sue you for libel,' he said. 'Emily never told us any of those things about him.'

'Emily was my sister,' Beattie retorted—they all spoke of her in the past tense now, 'I suppose I know what my own sister thought.'

One of the things that emerged was the fact that Stephen carried a handsome insurance on his wife's life.

'Well, he has to be a good advertisement for his job,' protested George. He thought sometimes it was a good thing Emily was dead somewhere or other—that, at least, he never doubted—because he might have been tempted to strangle her himself. Young Spence did a roaring trade, the shop had never had it so good; he was tougher than Stephen would have been.

'If you've come for a pinch of arsenic for your old man you've called at the wrong address,' he assured Mrs. Rorke, who was like the police in that she didn't intend to leave one stone upon another if she had a chance of dislodging it.

'This is a chemist's, not the gossip column,' he'd say, when other customers came prancing in to ask for three penn'orth of this or that, hoping for a pounds-worth of information.

His girl, Harry, was due for a week's leave about this time, and he hauled her into the shop as assistant. 'May as well learn the ropes while you get the chance,' he told her. He wasn't going to have a wife who went out to work, not unless she was working for him.

And then, when the hoo-ha was beginning to die down, because there's a time limit about these things and even corpses have to regard it, Emily surfaced.

CHAPTER VII

THE river had had her, after all. It had not treated her gently. The official view was that she had been plunged in by the weir and swept downstream. There was a tremendous drop in the water just below the weir and the authorities had erected a wall to prevent the unguarded from committing suicide. At this place the water sent up a fine endless spray like smoke, so that strangers, perceiving it from a distance, would wonder what on earth a steam train could be doing in that locality. At the foot of this drop the rocks thrust out like irregular teeth, and it seemed obvious that the unfortunate Emily had been battered among them, caught perhaps at the foot of the gorge and finally released by the rushing waters. When they got her out she was a dreadful spectacle, so fearfully injured and mutilated that even the police surgeon sniffed brusquely, saying, 'Where's the husband who's going to acknowledge that?' But there could be no doubt that it was Emily Tate. The dentures were still in place—'Not surprising,' said young Spence who appeared without respect for living or dead, 'seeing she kept her mouth clenched like a rat-trap whenever she wasn't speaking,' and these were identified by her dentist. Also by some odd trick the spare ear-ring was still in the ear, which had been pierced years ago; her hair had been swept over this ear giving it some protection, though the clothes were mostly swept away. It was possible to ascertain the cause of death and this was not drowning, but due to dislocation of the spinal column. If she had been wearing a scarf, her assailant might have caught both ends and drawn them tight, thus causing almost instant asphyxiation. It was less easy to say whether there had been a struggle, the injuries being so widely spread.

But of one thing they were certain. The victim had been dead before she was put into the water.

Lily learned the news over the radio. And not long afterwards she learned what everyone else had been anticipating for days, ever since the hunt was up, in short, that Stephen Tate had been arrested for the murder of his wife, Emily.

There are commonly held to be two main reasons for murder—passion and greed. The first was already in evidence, and when the authorities made a more detailed search of the house they found a will, in a secret drawer in a bureau in the dead woman's room. This had been drawn up on a printed form and witnessed by Jessie Leach and Elizabeth Leach, names that Stephen swore meant nothing to him. But when the fact became known two elderly sisters came forward to say that some months earlier they had been passing through Little Wyvern and had stopped at the chemist's to get some frozen eau-de-Cologne for one of them to alleviate a sick headache. They had been served by Emily who had told them what to look for in the church, and had then asked if they would do her a favour. She wanted, she explained, a paper witnessed, adding that she could not ask her husband or her assistant. They had realised, of course, that the document was a will, had signed and thought no more of it. When it was known that Emily Tate was missing they hadn't associated her with the woman in the chemist's shop. They explained they made a point of not reading about murders or any crimes of violence, and in any case the name over the shop being Purdy would have misled them. True, there had been a photograph of Emily fairly widely published but even Stephen had looked a bit dubious when he saw it. They couldn't have helped the police, they protested, since they didn't know what was in the will. And what was in the will came as a shock to everyone. Emily had left her personal belongings to her sister, a bequest to the local church, and the shop, goodwill and stock to Peter Spence, on condition that he was still in her employ.

'Blow me down!' said young Spence, reverently. 'So that's what she meant when she said patience pays off. Mind you, she didn't mean to die for another twenty years, and she'd have kept me dangling all that time.' Most likely, he confided to his Harry, she hadn't expected him to stay the course. It was just a way of paying out Stephen. So it looked as though she'd suspected the truth about Lily all along.

The police went further. They thought it was pretty good proof she must have known, and that was fuel to the faggots that were being piled round the widower's stake. Stephen could protest that she'd known nothing, that she couldn't have known and kept silent; Lily could swear till she was blue in the face that the news had come as a blinding shock, but no one had to believe them, and not many people did. Even Arthur Crook was inclined to reserve judgment.

It was Lily, that unobtrusive creature, so remote from the violent side of existence that you could almost forget she was breathing, who brought Crook into the case. As soon as she heard the news she sent Stephen the first letter she had ever written to him. They had been madly careful, and though Stephen had occasionally put pen to paper, relieving his burdened heart, she had refrained. Wives, she knew, sometimes go through their husband's pockets, and Stephen might not have the heart or the good sense to destroy a lover's letter.

'You will need a lawyer,' she wrote. 'Don't accept any offer that may be made you, I know the man you must have, and I shall get him for you. Don't trouble yourself about money, I have savings and my expenses have always been small.'

When she had posted the letter she put on her best clothes and went out of the house for the first time since the trouble broke. To the Press, who wanted a statement, she said coolly, 'You can tell them Arthur Crook will be acting for Mr. Tate. I am on my way now to make the necessary arrangements.'

She spoke with absolute conviction. No one asked her how she had heard of Crook or why she was so certain that he would undertake to work for Stephen, but one reporter observed to another, 'If I was in Crook's shoes I'd take it, too. Who was the chap who said the female of the species is more deadly than the male? I tell you, that fellow knew his onions.'

Mr. Arthur Crook, least conventional of lawyers, sat in his eyrie of an office at 123 Bloomsbury Street and observed to Bill Parsons, his invaluable A.D.C. 'Another husband payin' the price. You would think, seeing they've been in the noose all these years, the Crown 'ud make allowances, give 'em a bit of a discount like, but no. Still, there's one thing,' he went on cheerfully, 'he can't be nagged while he's in durance vile, and warders, being mostly married men, will probably feel sorry for him. Do the same thing themselves, I dare say, some of 'em, if they dared.'

He was working on a puzzler that was defying even his ingenuity when Bill put his head round the door inquiring, 'Time for a new client?'

Mr. Crook joyfully pushed his papers aside. 'I'm like the monk in that poem we used to learn at school—"though I be poor, I never turned a suppliant from my door," or words to that effect. Who is it, Bill?'

'The unofficial Mrs. Stephen Tate,' Bill told him.

'She hasn't wasted her time. O.K., Bill, shove her in.'

Lily entered, not too tall, slenderly built (Crook liked 'em plump when he could be said to like them at all), with a cloud of dark hair round a thin, closed face. He realised that she was dressed in her Sunday best, a dark suit, an unaccustomed hat (he knew it was unaccustomed because of the way she kept putting up a hand to touch it), kid gloves that she peeled off and rolled into a neat ball, as she took the chair he offered her, probably the most uncomfortable chair in a radius of twenty miles.

'I had to come,' she said instantly. 'I told Stephen I would be getting you for the defence.'

'You've come to the right shop,' said Crook, heartily. 'Now, let's suppose I don't know a thing about this, and that's a fact. That is, I only know what I've seen in the Press, and the little they've revealed you'd think rationing was back amongst us.'

She told her story with a simple directness that put him instantly on her side, starting with their first meeting at the obscure country hotel.

'Of course, I never dreamed then what would happen,' she said.

'I should hope not,' said Crook, severely. 'If you began with murder in mind . . .'

'I didn't mean that. I meant that the miracle should happen to him, too.'

Crook thought he could have found a more appropriate word than miracle, but janes were like that. Enthusiasm burnt out the fine flame of reason, and he could see from the start that he and she were two of a kind. What concerned her wasn't whether her beloved Stephen had killed his wife—she'd justify that to St. Peter himself—no, all she cared about was that he should get free and come back to her. Probably one of those maniacs who really would think it a privilege to be allowed to work her fingers to the bone for the man she loved.

'It didn't seem possible Emily shouldn't see the change in him,' she continued. 'And that being so, how could she want to keep a man who was in love with someone else?'

'Not speaking from experience,' said Mr. Crook, modestly, 'I'm told wives can be very disobliging in these circumstances. Could be that matrimony has rubbed the gilt off the gingerbread and they've stopped believing in romance.'

'I wanted Stephen to tell her at once, and when he kept putting it off I thought . . .' she hesitated.

'You thought the grey mare was the better horse and you could do a better job than him,' supplemented Crook in his usual ungrammatical fashion.

'I thought I could make her understand. I didn't know. Mr. Crook, if she treated him in the way she spoke to me—then there should be a verdict of justifiable homicide, even if he did kill her.'

'Here, take it easy,' Crook expostulated. He took pretty high fences himself, but here was a woman who practised a sort of moral levitation that left him gasping. 'You can't put your old woman undergound because of a difference of opinion. The morticians 'ud be working all round the clock if that were so.'

'Things happen so fast,' she pleaded. 'You're presented with a *fait accompli* almost before you realise what's happening. And there was that letter . . .'

'Remember, I'm new to this case,' Crook warned her. 'What letter was that?'

'You must have read about that in the paper. The letter—well, note really—he found when he got back.'

'In your Stephen's place, I'd play that letter down a bit,' Crook advised. 'Y'see, a jury's going to argue that when a dame plans to leave her ever-loving, she's inclined to spread herself a bit, firstly, secondly, and so on, and a scrap of paper with no beginning and no formal signature, as if she was putting out a note for the milkman, is going to make even them open their big sleepy eyes. And then, of course, they'll argue they've had their little matrimonial squabbles, too, and it's never driven them to picking up an axe or what-have-you; and the ones that aren't married aren't much better; they'll know that come what might they'd never succumb to temptation. If I was the prosecution I'd be inclined to ask just when Stephen first saw that letter. Say she'd cottoned on to what was afoot—she had cut him out of her will, remember, she could have written to him in just those terms, he comes back a day early to have it out with her, the lady ain't exactly complimentary to you, and he tells her to shut her big mouth. When she don't take the hint, he shuts it for her. So there he is, faced with a corpse. What's he to do with it? Answer—give the impression she's gone of her own accord. He can't leave it there and suggest suicide, because it ain't so easy to break your own neck, but there's that letter in his breast pocket . . .' carried away by his own eloquence Mr. Crook actually began to fumble in his own breast pocket—'tear the sheet in half and it'll do a treat. Ditch the car, pop the body over the weir—it don't seem to have occurred to him that doctors can tell if a body's drowned or no, water in the lungs, see—trail back along the riverside—it must have been a shock to him to meet a rozzer, but up he pops with this yarn about a bird no one else has ever heard of—and "Just imagine, Inspector, my wife's walked out on me." Just suppose it wasn't your Steve, how would it seem to you then?'

'He might have killed her,' agreed Lily, stubbornly, 'though he's not naturally a violent man, but he couldn't have acted all that, I'm certain.'

Crook was eyeing her thoughtfully. 'Now your story,' he suggested. 'Didn't leave out the tailpiece or anything? I mean, the lady was still rarin' to go when you left the house?'

'Oh, yes, Mr. Crook. She was furious. There's no doubt she hadn't suspected, she didn't recognise my name and I'm sure she didn't know why I should be calling, till I told her, I mean. And then—I don't think I'd have been surprised if she'd tried to throttle me herself. She made me think of that piece in the Bible about men calling on the rocks to fall down and cover them. It was like suddenly bumping up against a mountain.'

'Now, come, sugar,' Crook protested. 'I can draw the long bow with the best of them, but you want to stick to a *soupçon* of fact. If it had come to a shemozzle, well, you could give her twenty years and about three inches, so if one of you had come to harm, most people's money would have been on you.'

Lily shook her head. 'She could have broken me in half,' she assured him, simply. 'I can still feel those enormous hands, and her face pushing itself into mine. . . .'

'Sure we're talking about the same woman?' inquired Crook, politely. He picked up a paper from his desk. 'I admit she looks a tough nut, but she's in the bantam class all right.'

Lily took the paper from his hand. 'Who is this?'

'Now, don't play the innocent with me, sugar. That's Emily Tate. As if you didn't know.'

'It may be,' Lily agreed. 'I never saw her. You see, Mr. Crook, that's not the woman who opened the door of The Spinney to me the day Emily Tate disappeared.'

There was a moment's pause. Crook lighted another of his horrid little black cigars. 'That's a lovely curtain line,' he congratulated her. 'I can see it's going to be a privilege to work with you. Well,' he settled back cosily in his shabby old chair, 'seeing it wasn't

Mrs. Tate, the one you saw, any notion who it might have been?'

'Well!' Lily looked startled at such obtuseness. 'She was the murderer, of course. No wonder she wouldn't let me come any farther than the doorway.'

'It's a first-chop idea,' Crook agreed. 'Pity is you've let your bunny out of the hat a bit late in the day. The police are going to want to know why you didn't say your little piece when this picture first appeared.'

'But I never saw it till now,' Lily protested. 'I haven't been having a paper. I generally collect it, you see, but I haven't been going down to the village, and that picture wasn't in when the case was first reported.'

'It was on television,' Crook reminded her.

'I don't have a set.'

'Oh, well,' warned Mr. Candid Crook, 'I might believe you, but thousands wouldn't. Would you know her again?'

'I never really saw her properly. The hall was dark and she terrified me so—all I could tell was that she was a big woman and fairer than Emily's made out to be. She was wearing a hat and gloves—I did think that was odd, in her own house, but I suppose she'd only just got back.'

'You don't read enough whodunnits,' Crook told her kindly. 'Everyone knows about criminals wearing gloves by this time.'

'But if she did kill Emily—it seems funny to strangle someone when you were wearing gloves.'

'Who says she did? Probably put them on later. Wouldn't you?'

'Because of fingerprints. Did the police find any?'

'They didn't get the chance. Your Steve saw to that. Ran round with a polishing duster once he knew you'd come calling—the button put him on the track, remember, and though he didn't find it till the inspector pointed it out to him that night, that still gave him plenty of time—and if he had overlooked anything his Mrs. Mopp came in the next morning.'

'Yes, of course. Mr. Crook, do you suppose the woman I saw was A. M.?'

'Well, it ain't actually been established there's any such person. Yes, I know about the envelope, but anyone can type an address and tear the envelope in half and leave one bit in the basket all ready for the rozzers. And has anyone come forward who remembers her?'

'That's only one side of the coin,' Lily insisted. Stephen would have been amazed to see the transformation of his gentle love. 'No one can say she doesn't exist. Just because Mrs. Rodding at Curtonbridge Street doesn't remember her, that doesn't prove a thing. She has any number of letters sent there, and she has customers coming in for cigarettes and papers, why should she remember one particular correspondent? I mean, there's no proof that Emily Tate ever visited the shop.'

'That's what I said. Mrs. R. must have been shown a photograph and said she didn't recognise it.'

'But why should Emily go there? She had her own house and Stephen was away all the week. There could be no danger to her having letters sent to The Spinney. And since no one knew what A. M. looked like, how could you expect Mrs. Rodding to remember her?'

Crook considered. 'You've got a point there. But it would be better still if we knew a bit more about the lady you surprised that afternoon. Big, hands like a butcher, inclined to be fair, wearing a hat—anything special about the hat?'

'I didn't notice. Anyway it was pretty dark.'

'So where do we go from here?' Crook speculated.

'But we do know something,' Lily argued. 'We know she could drive a car, because of course Emily Tate never piled up her own car where it was found, and she must know the neighbourhood or she wouldn't have known about that place in the woods, and she hasn't got an alibi for midday Thursday.'

'I'll tell you what we don't know,' said Crook, 'and that is why Emily should be the corpse and not A. M. It wasn't particularly clever to kill the goose that laid the golden eggs.'

'Unless Emily had threatened to go to the police.'

Crook shook his head. 'You don't miss a trick, do you? Only if Emily was going to threaten her with the police it would have been before she started paying out the money. I mean, it 'ud have been honours even, neither of 'em able to make a move because of what the other one might say. No, you'd have expected A. M. to be the candidate for the Cemetery Stakes instead of *vice versa*.'

Lily took it all in her stride. 'Perhaps that's the way it was meant to be. Emily asks A. M. to come over, perhaps she meant to poison her or something. . . .'

'And leave the body lying on the floor? Bit awkward, don't you think?'

'You don't have to die on the spot,' Lily urged. 'It could be something that didn't work for an hour or so. Then she'd be well away from The Spinney. And she can't have taken anyone into her confidence, A. M., I mean, because if she had that person would have come forward. What surprises me is that she didn't just leave Emily at The Spinney. Then someone else would have found her.'

'Bit awkward if Mrs. Mopp came peeping through the windows and saw the body on the floor and let out a yell, and Stephen, so far as anyone knew, half the world away. Besides, amateurs never have the sense to let well alone, they must tie up all the ends, and they're probably brought to book because some Nosey Parker recognises their particular way of tying a knot. By the way, I take it you've got Stephen's power of attorney.'

The quick flush ran into her thin cheeks. 'If you were thinking about your fee . . .'

'I wasn't,' said Crook, truthfully. 'Only I don't want to go down and find he's got everything tied up with some other body.'

But he saw from Lily's face that he was wasting his breath. She might be the angel Stephen secretly thought her, but that didn't stop her being a woman in love, who knew what was best and stop her if you dare.

'Not me,' said Mr. Crook. 'I'm one of those unpredictable chaps that like staying alive.'

After Lily had gone, he told Bill he might try his hand at the problem that had been exercising his (Crook's) wits when Lily surfaced. He and the Superb, his famous ancient yellow Rolls, were on their way to a new case.

Little Wyvern drowsed in the unexpected sun. In the chemist's shop in the High Street a smart, pretty girl with her hair drawn up like a Roman helmet stood behind the counter; young Spence was partially concealed behind a glass panel, making up prescriptions. When Crook came whirling in like a brown-tweed Boreas the girl said composedly, 'What can I get for you?'

And he replied, 'I'm in here for info. to-day.'

'No Press in working hours,' announced the invisible voice. Young Spence had moved to open the drug cabinet.

'I'm not the Press,' reproved Mr. Crook. 'You must be wearing black glasses.'

'Crime writer wanting to verify details of a poison plot?' guessed the young man, coming out of hiding. 'We charge for info. like anything else here.'

Crook hauled a card out of his pocket. Spence took it, read it, grinned.

'Well, well, well,' he remarked. (It was obvious that the virtue of reverence had been left out of him at his christening.) 'The Bloomsbury Wonder in person. What brings you on the scene? No, don't tell me. You're going to prove Emily Tate killed herself and laid a trail to land her husband on the gallows. Well, if she did, she didn't confide in me.'

'Don't blame her,' said Crook, rudely. 'I'd as soon put tea in a leaky bag. Can't Sugar here hold the fort for five minutes,' he wheedled, 'while you put me in the picture? I see you've got a snug little sanctum back there.'

'Must have Sam Weller eyes,' said Peter Spence. 'O.K. I suppose if I was a cautious chap I'd frisk you first, but Chance is my middle name.'

'How does it feel to be your own boss?' queried Crook as the door closed behind them.

'That'll be the day. It appears, till the little matter of Emily's demise is cleared up, the cautious old men of law won't move. I say, you haven't come to tell me there's a hole in the will?'

'It can be as full of holes as a colander for me,' retorted Crook in his hearty fashion. 'Did she ever mention her intentions?'

'Well, in the sort of round-the-corner-and-up-the-alley way women do.' Young Spence struck an attitude. ' "Well, no, dear, it wasn't green and it wasn't blue, and not really grey," he announced in a mincing falsetto voice, "a kind of mixture of all three." ' His voice dropped several tones, he answered himself, and now a deep treacly note infused his speech. ' "I know exactly what you mean dear." Which is more,' added Spence reverting to his own voice, 'than any man could. What happens when they go into shops to match something up beats me.' He sketched a lightning impression of a bewildered shopkeeper hauling down bolts of coloured cloth.

'You're wasted behind a counter,' Crook assured him. 'I'd say Thespian rather than Chance was your middle name.'

'In point of fact and strictly between ourselves it's Surbiton, after an uncle who failed to brass up as expected. Married when he was seventy-plus, the dirty old man, and the widow scoffed the lot. Can you beat it?'

'P.S.S.' grinned Crook. 'Your parents must have had a sense of humour.'

'I've wondered about that. Well, fourteen years and not a hint of the patter of baby feet and then me and then my sister, Ruth. Now, just what do you want from me, Mr. Crook?'

'I represent the defence,' announced Crook, and like a flash came the retort, 'Lumme, he must be in a bad way. You mostly take 'em over on their death-beds, don't you? Well, come on. Are you here to buy my evidence or what?'

'What,' agreed Crook. 'I've seen your statement to the police. You went round about one-thirty and heard voices, gab, gab.'

'The wireless,' Spence reminded him. 'And one-thirty 'ud be about right. Amazing how many citizens want to play last across the road about twelve fifty-nine p.m. on a Thursday. Snatched a coffee and an ersatz hamburger, got the word from my second-best girl-friend and went beetling round to The Spinney. But no soap, I told the police that.'

'Now, cast your mind back,' Crook urged. 'I know the wireless was playing, but—no unrecorded voices? Two ladies having a bit of an argy-bargy?'

'They could have been collecting their breath for the next thrilling instalment, I suppose. All that yaketty-yak must ruin their throats. Not surprising the sale of pastilles is going up like a jet fighter. But no, Mr. Crook, I didn't hear any voices I could swear were being done straight.'

'The car?' Crook suggested. 'Ready to swear it was Mrs. Tate's?'

'It's like yours,' returned Spence frankly. 'There can't be two like it in the world. Car, typewriter, clothes—any museum 'ud be glad of them. "Why don't you turn it in?" I'd asked her. "My brother-in-law's in the trade, he'd get you special terms." But no. Might as well try to shift the Rock of Ages. Y'know, you can't blame Stephen Tate for letting his fancy wander. After living alongside a dingy little sparrow like that for years he'd be bound to be dazzled by a Bird of Paradise.'

'That how she struck you?' commented Crook, casually.

'Mark you, it wasn't her get-up or her make-up, they were both as quiet as the evening bell, but a kind of inner light. And all shined up for Stephen Tate. It's rum what women fall for.'

'I'd noticed that myself,' said Crook.

'Personal? Oh, well, I've always believed in miracles, and then a nice girl like Harry wouldn't want to be responsible for a man's death. There was a chap hanging round her, and I just put it to him he'd look even better hanging from a lamp-post and he vanished like a pantomime fairy. Now, let's come to the point. For all I know Harry's poisoned half a dozen profitable customers by this time.'

'I thought you said you didn't see anyone that afternoon. So how come you know the lady looked like a Bird of Paradise?'

'Oh, I didn't see her that day. No, it was a rum thing. He never opened his mouth about her, of course, but Harry and I go in for amateur theatricals, makes a nice change being the wicked uncle or the satin-slippered sleuth.' He whirled a pipe out of his pocket with a gesture that wouldn't have disgraced a TV production. ' "Hands up, or I fire" you know, all the trimmings. Well, we were going a bit far afield to oblige my sister who had some charity do and couldn't find anyone else dumb enough not even to charge expenses, and en route the car got held up by lights; and there was a car coming the other way and blow me down, there was Mr. Emily Purdy at the wheel and the Bird of Paradise perched alongside. If Emily could have seen him! Still, I dare say she wouldn't have recognised him. I hardly knew him myself. The frog that turned into Prince Charming wasn't in it.'

'So that's how you knew! I wondered. Happen to mention it to anyone?'

'Only the inspector when he came nosing round that evening, and then it sort of slipped out. Mind you, I didn't know who she was or her address or anything. No idea, then, of course, that Madam was already swimming under water.'

'And you didn't see anyone coming or going?' Crook persisted.

'That Thursday? No. Well, they were all inside scoffing lunch. I came by the short cut at the back, I suppose there could have been someone in the front though they'd vamoosed by the time I got round to pull the bell like an honest-to-god visitor. No answer there so I went round to the back. I knew she must be in because of the car. She didn't walk out to post a letter if she could help it. I called it a day at last, and decided to tackle her at six o'clock when she came round to the shop. I knew they couldn't do anything about the lease, because the place closed on Thursdays. Still, my idea is she was probably a goner by two, because I put in a call from the booth on the Green and no one answered, and don't tell me there's a woman living will let a phone ring if she's got even one leg left to hop to it. What makes you think there could have been someone else on the premises?' he added.

'That's a silly question. We know there was someone else on the premises, because Mrs. Tate didn't put herself in the river, and it can't have been Stephen Tate because I'm working for him, and the same goes for the Bird of Paradise. Besides, she saw another woman.'

'Come up a bit late with that notion, hasn't she?'

99

Crook explained.

'When did she get this idea?'

'In my office.'

Young Spence dug his hands in his pockets. 'Arthur Crook and his Bird of Paradise. Biggest juggling act in years. I hand it to you, Mr. Crook, you don't miss a trick. I wonder if I'd have thought of that if Harry had been in Stephen Tate's shoes.'

'You'll be in Emily Tate's shoes if you don't watch that tongue of yours,' Crook warned him quite pleasantly, but the young man stiffened abruptly.

'Well, sorry I can't help you,' he said in conciliatory tones, 'but it's God's truth I didn't see a soul. No eye, beady or bulging, peering round a curtain as I took my departure. Well, naturally I looked over my shoulder. Lady might have wanted to know who was calling.'

'Oh, well.' Crook stood up. 'I didn't really think you could tell me anything. I mean, you'd have bounced into the open long before this, wouldn't you? The Man Who Saw The Murderer.'

He turned towards the door. 'Sure we can't oblige with a tube of toothpaste or something?' urged the young man, hospitably. But Crook said, 'Not to-day, thanks,' and he didn't suppose anything in their bottles would appeal to him.

'I don't believe that man likes me,' said Spence wonderingly to the girl of his heart as the Superb bowled towards the Sitting Duck.

But it didn't stop there long. Crook bought a couple of pints for himself and one for Tom behind the bar and a fourth for a loquacious stranger, but it all added up to precisely nothing, so he rejoined the big yellow Rolls and they drove off to see if Stephen Tate could prove more amenable.

CHAPTER VIII

AFTER Lily's warmth and zest Stephen was like a douche of cold water. If he was startled by the appearance of his advocate nothing about him revealed the fact. He said in his sober way, 'Miss Vane told me to expect you.' He didn't have to say he'd never previously heard of Arthur Crook, because his face said that for him.

'How is she?' he went on, and Crook told him truthfully, 'If I was the one who put Mrs. Tate in the river I'd go into a nursing home for the next three months or see to it that she did.'

'That's what I'm afraid of,' said Stephen. 'I told her to keep out of this.'

'Your timing's wrong,' said Crook. 'She was in this before you were. There's only two choices. Either she knows a lot more about your wife's death than she's telling or she's actually set eyes on the murderer.'

He told Stephen what Lily had revealed to him. Stephen shook his head. 'She never said that to me.'

'She told you she'd been chucked out by your lady wife. Well, as it happens, that wasn't true, but she thought it was. It's a help in a way, because now we've good reason to believe there is such a person as A. M. All we knew before,' he added quickly, 'is that a torn envelope addressed to A. M. was found in the house, and that envelope was typed on your wife's machine. Now we know—at least you and I do—that there was a third party that afternoon. You can't recall anyone in your wife's life it might have been?'

'I never thought of Emily as a person with many friends. Even in Mr. Purdy's day everything was very quiet. They were both occupied with the shop during the week, and they were what you'd call Sabbatarians, no jollities on Sundays, no work either. Emily couldn't touch the accounts or a business letter, nothing. They never drank or smoked and not many people came in, and those that did were mostly for the old man. Of course, I'm away all week myself, but I hardly ever remember Emily having a friend in at the week-end. Believe it or not, but, even when he was ill and couldn't get out, Mr. Purdy wouldn't have the wireless on on a Sunday except for a service or a sacred concert.'

Crook nodded. For himself, he subscribed to the philosophy of the better the day the better the deed, but still, he could respect the old man's point of view if he couldn't share it. Life over the shop must have been a riot, and life at The Spinney didn't sound as if it had been much gayer.

'Tell me this,' Crook went on. 'What are you pleading?'

'Pleading?' Stephen gobbled. 'Innocent, of course.'

'Ah, but innocent of what? Murder? Manslaughter? Accessory before the fact? Now, remember I'm your friend, put all your cards on the table and I'll drop the ones we don't need in the wastepaper basket. When you came back to The Spinney that Thursday afternoon, did you find the body of your late lamented on the premises?'

'Well, of course I didn't.' Stephen sounded stupefied. 'I've told the police . . .'

'Ah, but I'm not the police. But say you had found the lady past help . . .'

'I should have telephoned to the authorities—naturally, I would.'

'Well, if you had any sense, and if you could prove you'd only just arrived. Could you?'

'I came by train—I had to change at London. I didn't see anyone I knew, but that's nothing special. I walked in from Chelston Station, the buses are impossible on Market Day.'

'Any proof what time you left wherever you were coming from? See what I mean? After all, there was the button to prove your young lady had been there. . . .'

'You're forgetting, it wasn't I who found the button. It was

Marston the same evening. If I'd found it, you don't imagine I'd have left it there.'

'What would you have done?'

'Well, I suppose I'd have gone up as soon as I could to see Lily and find out what had happened. I couldn't guess I was going to meet Mr. Marston down by the river. After that, I really hadn't any choice, I had to tell him Emily had gone.'

'Had to ask him in and show him the letter?'

'Well, it was proof, wasn't it?'

'He might argue that was why. Mind you, it does sound a bit rum that the minute you learn your wife's left you you clap on your deerstalker and go bird-watching.'

'There was nothing I could do in the house. I'd no reason to suppose she hadn't just walked out as her note said. You don't ring up the police to advertise the fact that your wife's left you. I mean, it's not a crime. Telling him to his face was different. It was bound to come out and it would have looked odd if I hadn't mentioned it. But surely, Mr. Crook, now we know there was someone else on the premises, don't I get the benefit of the doubt?'

'What we know don't cut any ice at all, it's what we can persuade the police to believe. So far nobody saw this mysterious dame except your Lily. It won't weaken the Prosecution's case until we can put up a bit of proven evidence. They believe you had a row, strangled Mrs. T., and disposed of the body. You were coming up from the river . . .'

'Do they really think I'd risk taking a body to the weir while there was still a beam of daylight?'

'You could have been surveying the landscape o'er, I suppose. There was the suitcase and the handbag—and there was the fact that you were seen burning the midnight oil in your kitchen. And you were seen the second time by Inspector Marston coming away from the river—you can't blame the police for counting a bit on their fingers.'

'That would suggest Emily was still on the premises when Marston came to the house.'

'Not exactly on the premises. You had locked the garage. Why were you in such a bait about finding the key that night?'

'I wanted to mend a puncture. That's why I was so late. I worked in the garage, there's no window, it's no more than a shed. When I'd finished I went into the kitchen to have some beer, and presently I went upstairs.'

'I don't know how long it usually takes to mend a puncture . . .'

'Depends how soon you can find it. In any case I didn't fancy going up right away. It's different for you, Mr. Crook, you're not a married man.'

'You're right,' said Crook, 'but what makes you so sure?'

'A married man sooner or later always mentions his wife. You haven't said a word. What I mean is an empty house is all right when you're single, but when you know you're alone because your wife can't stand the idea of stopping with you . . .'

'Draw it mild,' Crook advised him.

'Well, it's not much of a compliment to me that she couldn't confide in me, not after more than twelve years. I feel it very much, Mr. Crook.'

'You weren't being so hot on the confidence lay yourself,' Crook reminded him.

'I was going to tell her, I had to tell her.'

'Maybe. Now the Prosecution ain't going to take kindly to your idea that first you mended your bike and then you sat round solitary-like in the kitchen till one a.m.'

'What are they going to suggest I did?'

'I've had a butchers at your place,' Crook told him. 'There's a nice back path down to the river, wide enough to take a car, no traffic about that hour of the night, and if you should be seen goin' into the garage, well, there's your bike leaning against the wall . . .'

'And Emily's car alongside it?'

'I didn't mean the garage wall. I reckon you'd keep that locked up—I mean, they'll reckon it.'

'And Emily was there all the time I had the inspector in the house?'

'That 'ud be playing it smart. And the light was on at one a.m. Plenty of time to be sorting papers and doing a bit of clearing and cleaning up. And, of course, you've admitted you didn't know about the new will leaving the place to young Spence.'

Stephen's voice sounded choked. 'That was a spiteful thing to do.'

Crook shrugged. 'You didn't play your cards right there. You had the chance to be manager. Well, if you want to blame someone,' he burst out, 'blame the old man. It was up to him to put your name in his will if he had a mind.'

'We don't know he hadn't a mind. I've always wondered about Emily not sending for me at the end. It wasn't expected so suddenly, she said, but I was the only son he ever had, you'd think anyone would send for a son.'

'You think he asked for you and Emily didn't pass the message on?'

'We know he couldn't write, well, not a letter anyway. But she could have written for him.'

'But she didn't—why?'

'May not have wanted me to hear what he had to say, suppose he wanted a lawyer. . . .'

'He could have asked that old boy—what's his name?—Mainprice—to send for one.'

'I've thought about that. I've thought a lot.'

'All this thinking, never know where it'll lead you. Come on, what gives?'

'When you're in my shoes you haven't much to do but think. He wanted to see Mainprice specially, even Emily couldn't keep him out. I asked her afterwards if there was anything wrong at the shop, and she said, "No, the receipts were as high as ever", so why did he want to see him?'

'Make known his last will and testament? Is that your idea?'

'It could be.'

'Then why didn't Mainprice write?'

'It ties up with something else, Mr. Crook. Why did Emily make Mr. Mainprice her manager?'

'Daddy's dying wish perhaps.'

'No, it couldn't be that, because she wanted to have me for the job, it was only after I wouldn't take it on she got Mainprice. And she hadn't meant to have him. She practically said as much. She meant the business to be in our two hands—well, four hands. Get a young chap for counter-work—and as I say, I didn't think it was good enough. And when I came back the next week she said she'd decided to give Mainprice the job. No reason given that any sensible person could accept. People were used to him, she said, and at his age he wasn't likely to get anything else. No, the way I see it it was a bargain. "How do I stand if you and Mr. Tate get the shop?" he asks. "Do I stay on?" Well, I can tell you the answer to that, Mr. Crook. A month's notice. After all, a shop's a business, not a charity. If it hadn't been for the war, when you couldn't get anyone, even the girls were in uniform or the factories, he wouldn't have lasted a month. He and Louie had been bombed out from London and got re-settled here—he'd been a clerk in a pharmaceutical store, and remembering his age that speaks for itself. A chap who's a clerk at past sixty, and never been any better, mark you, what sort of a manager is he going to make for a going concern? I reminded Emily of that, she said she'd be the boss, and since I wouldn't take over myself, what concern was it of mine?'

'She had you there,' suggested Crook.

'And she was the one who was against him at the start, said she could manage on her own, but Mr. Purdy wouldn't have it. There were the books and the orders and the prescriptions and Mr. Purdy beginning to get his attacks of vertigo. Emily used to say it was enough to make you scream to watch him fumbling over orders she could have put up in half the time. She was a trained dispenser, could have got a job anywhere, but, of course, when you've got a family business you don't look to go outside, and it did get her off national service.'

'Even after Mainprice came? I thought they were scraping the bottom of the barrel by 1944.'

'The doctor gave her a certificate on Mr. Purdy's account, and it was true he could collapse at any time. Mind you, I didn't know them then, didn't know them at all till I got back from the war. No, she didn't keep Mainprice on of her own free will, and she didn't go on paying his pension, and helping Louie after the old man had gone, not without there was some pretty strong reason.'

'They were taking a chance. Suppose the old man had spoken of the will to anyone else?'

'Well, I don't see that he could, Mr. Crook. He never had any visitors, and when the doctor or the nurse was there Emily stayed in the room.'

'With Mainprice running the shop on his own?'

'They got a bit of part-time help, I understand, but no one stopped long. If there'd been any competition the shop must have suffered, but with half the buses cut off and no cars run for private business, people had to accept what offered. No, I can just hear the old man saying, "What if Louie and me was to forget about the will?" No proof of its existence beyond his word, of course, and I don't know how far that would have taken him in a court of law. On the other hand it wouldn't do Emily any good to have that kind of story floating round. The country isn't like London, everyone knows your business. But she must have paid, Mr. Crook, and not just in money. Because if there had been a will and it had been destroyed, well, no one but Emily could have done it. He never left his bed, couldn't even have got as far as the fire to burn it. For as long as he lived, Mainprice must have known he had Emily like that.' Stephen stretched out his big hand, palm upwards, and slowly closed his fist. 'She must have hated him, Mr. Crook, she never took kindly to dominance, not from anyone else, I mean.'

'Speaking as a husband?' Crook offered.

'I never tried. I mean, I knew the shop mattered more to her than I did. I've often thought she agreed to the marriage to please the old man as much as anything, and make sure she got the place afterwards. But I'd see her face sometimes when she sat sewing in a corner of an evening and he was laying down the law. Such a look on it—you could almost say hate. He liked his own way, too. You never saw him, of course. He was like a picture out of one of those old stories that came out in the Victorian magazines. My mother had some bound copies when I was a boy. A big rattling bag of bones, with a head like a skull, but very much all there. Eyes sunk back under eyebrows like a thatch, big hands—Emily must have taken after her mother—

like one of the minor Prophets, I used to think. I'd see him walk to church of a Sunday leaning on his big blackthorn stick —he read the lessons for years, and it 'ud curdle your blood to hear him chant the cursing psalms. Take their children and throw them against the stones, he'd cry. He was an honest man, wouldn't have cheated a penny on his income-tax or taken a thousand pounds for giving false witness or handing over something without a prescription, but a bad man to get up against. Still, his yea was yea and his nay, nay, and that's something in business, where half your clients seem to have been descended from eels.'

Crook was fascinated by his demeanour and the picture he painted. Under the surface quiet the flat above the shop must have seethed with suppressed emotion, with this big sober handsome chap the one real simpleton among them. For the first time he knew a pang of sympathy for Emily. Of course she had to fight for her own hand. Stephen was sold on Daddy, made no secret of the fact, and it's not much of a compliment to be married because Hubby likes the look of his father-in-law. It had never been the shop or what it promised that had attracted Stephen.

'How long did Mainprice last?' he inquired.

'Mr. Purdy died in 'fifty-one, and Mainprice hung on till about 'fifty-six. I wasn't having anything to do with the shop in those days, naturally. Then the old man had a stroke and the doctors told him he'd never go back behind the counter and Emily looked around and eventually she got this present young fellow. A very live wire, a bit too live for her I've sometimes thought. Emily went on calling the old man her absentee manager and she sent him his salary or a generous part of it. Early in 'fifty-seven he went to the hospital at Huntmere and Emily used to visit him. Louie moved down with him and got rooms near by. Well, it was lonely for her, the only girl being away.'

'Married, you said.'

'I've wondered about that sometimes. Louie and the old man shut up like clams whenever her name was mentioned. Could be she found her chap had a wife already or maybe he drank. I gathered they separated but she didn't come home. She didn't write often either, not so often as her mother thought she should, but everyone isn't handy with a pen. I mean, it comes natural to some and not to others.'

Crook shivered. The chap who wrote about single bliss had never uttered a truer word. The picture began to build up in his mind. He had never seen either of the protagonists, living or dead, but his imagination, that was considerably keener than most people appreciated, gave him a lightning vision of the pair— The Conspirators—two small bent heads practically knocking together. You scratch my back and I'll scratch yours. Silence is golden and gold fetches a big price these days. It had fetched Mainprice a manager's salary. All the same, something was missing. The old chap must have had some proof to keep Emily under his thumb for so long.

'When Mainprice died did Emily keep up with the widow?' he asked.

'She used to visit her regularly, helped her, too, I'm pretty certain. Mainprice was better at managing a business than his private affairs, she'd say, had the idea that Louie could live on the pension. Oh yes, she helped, I don't doubt. Still, the old lady didn't last long after Mainprice went, nothing to live for, you might say. And I suppose Emily thought she'd have a bit of peace at last.'

'And then A. M. turns up. What was the daughter's name?'

'Ida, Eileen, something like that. I told you, she went to South Africa.'

'And the tide at Southend goes half-way to France every day,' contributed Crook in oracular tones, 'but it comes in again. And daughters that go to South Africa sometimes come home.'

'She never came in her mother's lifetime,' Stephen insisted. 'I remember Emily saying once, "The poor old thing's as much alone as if she'd never had a husband or a child." '

Crook stood up. 'Well,' he said, 'thanks a million. I suppose you realise our net's got enough holes in it to let out anything smaller than a whale. We don't know the nature of Mainprice's hold over your late wife, it might have been a will, it might have been a bit of hanky-panky over the counter, it could have been something neither of us has thought of yet; we don't know that A. M. is anything to do with the Mainprices—what's the name of the landlady at Huntmere?'

Stephen thought. Crook realised for the first time the meaning of the phrase—Time stood still. Here it seemed frozen in its track. Then, like an aged cockroach, cautiously sticking out a feeler, he said, 'Mrs. Crabbe. That was it. Mrs. Crabbe.'

'Pity,' said Crook. 'Might have saved us a lot of trouble if it had been Melrose or Martin or Merrylegs. Well, I think my first step will be to have a word with her. If daughter did come back the odds are she'd have called at Huntmere, if only to see the grave. Yes, I know you said her name was Ida, but I dare say it could quite as easily have been Ada, couldn't it now?'

Stephen gave him a sickly smile and said, 'Well, perhaps it could.' Crook told him to keep his pecker up and bounced out. Some clients make a solicitor's job comparatively easy, want to help to carry the can. But not Stephen. He was like a dog who puts the ball at your feet and won't even nuzzle it with his nose. There's the ball, you throw it. Oh well, thought Crook, philosophically, me for the Olympic Games. If I can't chuck that ball and score a bull's-eye—his metaphors were inclined to be mixed, as became a man who hardly knew a hockey stick from a mashie.

Somerset House told him that a daughter had been born to Oswald and Louisa Mainprice forty-six years ago. No name had been given at the time of the registration and she simply appeared as a female infant, but Crook didn't feel even Fate could stretch the long arm of coincidence far enough to allow duplicate parents to have a daughter at more or less the same time. No, this was the one he was after. He asked for more information and learned that Ayleen Mainprice married Henry Smith, a native of South Africa, shortly before the war; after that there was no information. But that tallied with what he'd been told. They had gone to South Africa and more or less been lost on the veldt.

Me for Huntmere, decided Crook. He had achieved about a third of his journey before he realised that if Stephen hadn't been his client he'd be perfectly prepared to accept him as the guilty man. That shook him rather. He wasn't afraid of taking chances, holding that life's a tug-of-war for most people, between the police and the individual, but even he drew the line at murder. You had to admit that Stephen had had means, motive and opportunity and hadn't produced the flimsiest of alibis. He'd produced a fine cock-and-bull story about Mainprice and a missing will, but anyone who could have confirmed that or any part of it was now underground; and wouldn't a man who believed he was being defrauded of an inheritance have fought for it a bit harder? Which brought him to his next question—when precisely had Stephen thought up this story of the will? Had he spoken of it to Emily? He'd told Marston he'd always been convinced he should have inherited, but even to him he hadn't suggested that the will had actually existed and been destroyed.

Crook cheered himself up with the reflection that it was always a help to have an enterprising chap on your side, and the chances were roughly fifty-fifty and that was a better proposition than he'd often had to defend. Give him just a couple of trump cards, not find that this Mrs. Crabbe had sold up or followed her lodger to the churchyard and he—Crook—would surprise them all yet again. The only person he'd never succeeded in surprising was himself. In his heart of hearts he didn't believe he could lose.

CHAPTER IX

MRS. MABEL CRABBE of 3 Norman Road, Hunt-mere Chase, was at home when Crook called and reacted favourably at the mention of Louisa Mainprice. Yes, of course she recollected her, poor old thing, had stayed at Norman Road about two years, and then after the old gentleman passed over she seemed to lose interest.

'Interest in what?' asked Crook.

'Well, life, I suppose. Though, mind you, I thought it was funny.'

'Funny peculiar or funny ha-ha?'

'Funny peculiar. I mean, she was all strung up about the daughter coming home, and perhaps that's why she got excited and made the mistake.'

'What mistake?' asked Crook.

'Are you the police?' demanded Mrs. Crabbe.

'I'm trying to trace Mrs. Mainprice's daughter. I'm a lawyer,' he added smugly.

'Well, why couldn't you say? I can't give you her address because she didn't leave one. She'd only just arrived in England, see, didn't even know the old lady had gone.'

'Who sent for her? I take it she was expected?'

'She was expected all right. As soon as the old gentleman entered into his last phase—well, he was quite paralysed before the end, no power of speech, couldn't move, and no knowing whether he understood what was being said to him—well, like I was telling you, when he got to that stage Louisa wrote to her girl to come back.'

'Left it a bit late, didn't she?' suggested Crook. 'I mean, the old boy had been on his back for two years.'

'It wasn't him she was coming back to see. Louisa made that clear. In fact, he was the reason she stopped away so long. Live under my roof—never, that was his attitude.'

'He sounds a difficult old gentleman. Never come a cropper himself, I suppose.'

'I couldn't say. I know there's some believe the divine wrath only falls where it's merited, but I don't know about that. Louisa talked to me a bit because I was having trouble with my girl. Wanted to marry a beatnik if you please. "And what are you going to live on?" I asked her. "If you think I'll have a thing like that in my house. . . ." And she said, Louisa, I mean, "They never will listen, will they, they always know best. Mr. Mainprice and me could have told her that Smith was no good."'

'How no good?' asked Crook. 'I mean, couldn't he support her or had he already too many little Smiths and their Mum on his plate?'

'He deceived her,' said Mrs. Crabbe simply. 'That's what Louisa said to me. It wasn't her fault, she said, and if the girl took her own way out, well, people get desperate . . .'

'You can't mean she took Smith for a midnight swim and arranged a rendezvous with a croc?' suggested Crook, brilliantly.

'I'm sure she couldn't be blamed if she did,' flashed Mrs. Crabbe, 'but Louisa never said anything like that, and I'm not one to be nosy. Anyway, once Mr. Mainprice was at peace Louisa said she'd sent for Ayleen. "It'll be nice to have her with me again," she said. "I haven't seen her for nearly twenty years." And mightn't recognise her when you do meet, I thought, but naturally I didn't say anything. And, as it happened, it would have been a waste of breath.'

'Was Mrs. Mainprice's death a great surprise?'

'Well, naturally. Of course, she wasn't young, and it must have been trying waiting for Mr. Mainprice to go, but she was well cared for, and she didn't lack for anything. Mrs. Tate saw to that.'

'Mrs. Tate? She came visiting?'

'That's right. Louisa said Mrs. Tate owed a great deal to her husband after her father died—that 'ud be Mrs. Tate's father, I mean. Mr. Mainprice really kept the shop going, if it hadn't been for him Emily—she called her Emily—might have been ruined.'

'Not much of a business head?' murmured Crook.

'Well, she didn't say that, just what a standby Mr. Mainprice had been. Mrs. Tate used to visit and she always brought something, sent lovely flowers for the funeral and came herself, and afterwards her and Mrs. Mainprice had a long talk. I wondered if Louisa could manage the rent, because naturally his pension died with him, but it was all right. The best of everything she had. Chickens, cream, strawberries in season. I did for her, you understand, but she ordered her own meals. Mrs. Tate must have thought a lot of your husband, I said once, and she said, "There's some debts no money will repay."'

'Mr. Tate ever come?' asked Crook. 'I don't mean with her, but on his own.'

'Never to this house. Well, why should he? The business was nothing to do with him, and it wouldn't be very nice having a murderer on the premises.'

'Hold your horses,' advised Crook. 'No one's proved he's a murderer yet. Maybe Mrs. Tate was as nice to him as she was to your Louisa. How did they strike you, by the way? Great buddies?'

'Well, Louisa had her own little ways like old people do. Not that I saw a lot of them together. It was a chance for me to get out for a while. Louisa was getting a bit tottery, I did think sometimes she'd be better off in a home.'

'You don't mean that,' Crook corrected her, gently. 'You mean you'd be better off.'

'Of course when she said her daughter was coming back I stopped worrying. Though I did wonder how they'd hit it off, after all those years. Mrs. Tate was ever so sweet to her. "I'll be along next month," she'd say as she was going out, and "I'm sure you will, my dear," said Louie. No gratitude.'

'Gratitude's out,' said Crook. 'It's been exposed as a crawling servility. The best is good enough for you and you've a right to it. You were going to tell me about Mrs. Mainprice's death.'

'Yes. Well, she had been looking a bit pale, but I put that

down to excitement, her daughter coming back, see. And Mrs. Tate had said, "She seems a bit depressed, do you know if she's got anything on her mind?" I said, well losing your husband's always a bit of a shock, if it isn't always a grief, and she said she supposed so, and if Louie went on getting these headaches should she see a doctor? I said, well, she relied on aspirins, and they seemed to do her good, and perhaps she got a bit excited, having a visitor. Then Mrs. Tate said I suppose I'm her last link with the past. Mr. Mainprice worked for my father and afterwards for me, I expect she told you. I said, well, she'd told me what a lot you both owed to Mr. Mainprice, and after Mrs. Tate had gone I went in to see if I could get Louie any tea or anything. She had that and presently she ate a bit of the chicken Mrs. Tate had brought—and lovely flowers, she always brought flowers—and then she went to bed. And she never got up again and it's like I told the doctor, Mr. Crook, it was an accident, I know it was.'

'Go on,' said Crook, 'what happened? She didn't fall out of a window of anything?'

'Of course not. But she must have felt worse later on and she reached out for her aspirins.'

'Don't tell me,' said Crook. 'She picked up the wrong bottle. Couldn't she have put on the light?'

'Well, of course she could, but I suppose she was sleepy and didn't notice. I had warned her to be careful, they looked ever so alike, and of course more than one of her sleeping tablets would do the trick. But she'd never have done it on purpose, not with the girl coming home and all.'

'What was the result of the inquest?' Crook inquired.

'Oh, Dr. Murray was very good, he didn't let it come to an inquest. No one could believe Louie would take her own life, a God-fearing woman like her. I'm chapel myself, but I hope I can see the good in others. But the vicar's fussy and we didn't want a scandal, and Dr. Murray put heart failure on the certificate. He said she wouldn't have lasted long anyway.'

'What did you tell the daughter?' asked Crook with real curiosity.

'I told her what the doctor said. It was funny to think of her as Louisa's daughter, Louisa being so small. She was a big woman who must have been fair when she was a girl—well, Louisa always said her hair was her crowning glory—not badly dressed, mark you, but not elegant. Her mother seemed to get more pernickety as she got older, very nice things she had, the daughter told me to take my pick, but there, I'm on the big side, too. There was a lovely leather handbag I would have liked, Mrs. Tate brought it on Louie's birthday, but Mrs. Mainprice's Ayleen kept that. Well, hers was nothing, a plastic affair with gilt initials, and her clothes were just heavy tweed and a hat like a hen's nest. Mind you, she spoke very nicely of all I'd done for her mother, and she went to have a look at the grave, and when she came back she gave me a present and I gave her the letter Louie had left.'

Crook pricked up his big ears. 'How come she wrote a letter if she didn't know she wouldn't be there in person?' he inquired.

'Oh, this was just after she knew Ayleen was coming back. "No man knows when his hour approaches," she said, "and if anything should happen to me I want you to give this to my daughter." Sealed it was and all. There was a bit of money in the bank but apart from that there was nothing really. They'd sold up when Mr. Mainprice had to give up working.'

'Had anyone warned Ayleen that her mother was dead?' Crook wanted to know.

'The doctor thought of that. He asked me if I knew the name of the ship and he wrote a letter marked "Urgent". She just came with one little case, thinking she'd need to spend a night to see the bank and so forth. She didn't look too prosperous to me, that case had knocked about a lot, and she must have seen me looking at it because she said, "That's the case they gave me when I got married—there was J.S. painted on it—and I never bothered to change the initials. I don't call myself Mrs. Smith any more." She asked where her mother's things were . . .' Mrs. Crabbe stopped. 'There now, I was forgetting, there was one thing I thought a bit funny. Mrs. Tate came down for the funeral, of course, and she came to see me, as you'd expect. "I dare say you've had a lot of bother about this," she said. "Perhaps you'd like me to go through her papers and so forth, unless she's got a lawyer." She hadn't, of course, but I told her I thought it 'ud be best to wait till her daughter came back. "Daughter?" said Emily. "Is she expected?" So I said, "Didn't Louie tell you? She's on her way now, and I don't doubt she'd wish to find everything as her mother left it." Mrs. Tate said, "Well, of course, I didn't understand." But I did think it funny. Nosy, you know.'

'Nothing wrong with curiosity that I can see,' Crook defended the absent woman stoutly. 'If people hadn't got curious minds we'd still be in the Stone Age. Inventors,' he added.

Mrs. Crabbe sniffed. 'When you think the kinds of things they're inventing nowadays the Stone Age might be a lot safer,' she said.

'I suppose Ayleen didn't leave an address?' Crook hazarded, not wishing to become involved in an Atom Bomb discussion.

'She said she might be going to London. "Funny," she told me, "all these last years I've dreamed of London." "You'll find it a lot changed by all accounts," I told her. I believe she called to see the Vicar, but you don't get any change out of him, he said he thought tombstones were heathenish—everyone's got some bee buzzing in his bonnet—and she went along to the bank at Huntmere. And that's the last I saw of her.'

'Ask for Emily's address?'

'Well, yes, she did. Said she ought to thank her for being so good to her mother. I did wonder if she'd send me a postcard, but there hasn't been anything since.'

'When was all this?'

'When Mrs. Mainprice died? It was just before Christmas. "Well," I said to her daughter, "it's nice to think of them being together again for the family festival," but she said, "I'd like my mother's word for that."'

'So would I,' said Crook. 'Y'know, Mrs. Crabbe, there's times I wish I was a member of the Psychical Society and could get in touch with the dear departed. What they'd tell me 'ud probably turn my hair grey.'

For form's sake he called at the Vicarage but he didn't get anything there, and set out on the drive back. The rain had started in real earnest now, it was going to be a black night, and he couldn't think of many better places to spend it than the bar of the Duck. He became increasingly aware of a sense of unease, the kind of thing housewives know, inwardly convinced they've left the electric iron burning or a gas jet under a boiling cabbage. Somewhere along the road he had been handed a bit of information and he'd let it fall. This wouldn't have happened ten years ago, he thought. One of the penalties of Anno Domini. He had gone nearly thirty miles before the penny dropped. It mightn't mean a thing, but a man in his shoes couldn't afford to take a chance. He'd noticed that Mrs. Crabbe had no telephone, and he didn't imagine she was great on correspondence. With a huge groan he turned the Superb and went back to Huntmere Chase. The rain came shouting after him, like a chorus of defeat.

This time luck was against him. Mrs. Crabbe was not at home. Every small window was fastened and the curtains drawn; the little house had an air of idiot satisfaction, the kind of expression he associated with men who plume themselves on being total abstainers, say, a holier-than-thou look. He thought he'd like to kick the windows in. He walked uneasily to and fro for a minute in case she'd only run to the post, and then he was aware he was being watched from an adjacent house. He bounced through the little gate and up the two steps. The door was opened with such alacrity that he realised he was going to be pumped, and promptly went dry.

'Mrs. Crabbe be gone to chapel,' he was told.

'On a weekday?' (It was Thursday.) He groaned for the extravagance of women who know nothing of the happy mean. 'Likely to be long?'

The neighbour couldn't say. She attended the Methodists herself. Crook found out where Mrs. Crabbe's particular place of worship was situated and planted himself outside like some prehistoric yellow monster. It was nearly an hour before Mrs. Crabbe appeared in a flurry of women, all chattering and speculating and making plans. Like a blooming lot of hens, thought the unappreciative Mr. Crook, pecking at the grains, head down, gab, gab, dig, dig. He tooted imperiously on the horn, and they all looked up as startled as though the cock had suddenly surfaced. Crook climbed down and approached Mrs. Crabbe.

'Drive you back,' he offered.

'I'm going back with my friend,' said Mrs. Crabbe. 'She's got the television.'

Crook looked winningly at the friend, who might have been the original of Sairey Gamp. She said later she felt as if she were being surveyed by an alligator.

'Give me five minutes and I'll drive you both home,' he offered.

'Cost me nearly sixty miles to get this five minutes. Matter of life and death.'

The two women exchanged significant glances; obviously the minister had just used a similar expression, and grudgingly Mrs. Crabbe agreed.

'Those initials on the plastic handbag,' he said, 'were they the same as the ones on the suitcase?'

'Well, of course they weren't. It was a new bag. She said she wasn't calling herself Smith any more. And seeing how badly he treated her you couldn't expect her to want to go on using his name. And you could say she had a right to the other, even if it's not what you'd think to do yourself.'

'And the greatest of these is charity,' intoned Mr. Crook, slamming the door of the Superb and whirling her away. The friend had gone on; after the address they'd just heard she wasn't going to trust herself to a thing that looked like a yellow hearse.

The rain continued to fall, the wind rose. It was going to be a night that only the ducks would enjoy. Crook came striding into the bar of the Sitting Duck soon after opening time, calling for beer. When it was brought he tossed down a pint in one mighty swallow and demanded a refill. He was dealing with this in more leisurely fashion when Tom, coming through from the Private said, 'Mr. Crook, someone's been calling you.'

'Leave a name?' inquired Crook.

'Well, no.'

'Male or female?'

'Deep voice, a man I'd say.'

'Didn't recognise it, though?'

'Well!' Tom looked a bit injured. 'Just a voice on the line and nothing to show it's not a teetotaller. It's not reasonable.'

'Life ain't—reasonable, I mean. That's what's so unfair. Any message?'

'Just asked when you'd gone out and when you were expected back.'

'How long ago?'

Tom was a bit vague. Round about an hour, he thought, could be less.

'And you told him I'd been out most of the day. I see.'

'Probably ring again after opening time,' suggested Tom, encouragingly. He moved away to serve a couple who had just come in. Crook looked up and down the bar. An evening paper lay on the counter and he read the headlines upside down.

'How long's that been there?' he asked Tom when he came back. From his casual voice you'd never have guessed his heart was leaping like a fish.

'Matter of an hour,' hazarded Tom. 'Brought in from Chelston, I dare say. We don't get the evening papers here, not without they're ordered or come by post the next morning.'

'Talk about the outskirts of civilisation,' Crook groaned to himself.

The barman obligingly retrieved the discarded sheet and offered it to Crook. He read : New Clue in Village Mystery. Someone had unearthed the fact that there had been a third woman at The Spinney that fatal Thursday.

Crook finished his pint and gently returned the glass to the counter.

'This chap, the one who rang,' he said. 'If he should come through again, tell him I'm on my way.'

'Where's that?' asked Tom.

'He'll know. By the way, where's the telephone? I've got to ring a lady.'

Tom's eyebrows shot into his hair, but he led Crook into a narrow passage behind the bar. Crook dialled a number and stood there, hearing the bell ringing away in the dark with the forlornness of all unattended summonses. No one there, he guessed, but he let it ring on for twice the number of rings he usually allowed. But at last he hung up. His contact wasn't at home, and now time was the essence of the situation. He got through to the operator and asked for a London number, but it wasn't his lucky night. The storm, whose ferocity was momentarily increasing, had brought down the lines north of Little Wyvern, and as of now only local calls were available. So he came back to the bar and paid his shot and walked out of the door and into the Superb like a man in a dream.

'Taken the knock,' said a knowing fellow watching his progress. 'Wonder what sort of a woman it is could do that to him.'

CHAPTER X

At Periford Lily Vane sat in her blacked-out house as much a refugee as if she were a criminal for whom the police were searching. People knocked on the door, tapped on the window, even climbed over the little garden wall. But there was no way in; there were shutters at all the windows, and all the shutters were bolted.

It had been raining steadily since four o'clock. Lily, who hated the wet like a hen, a poodle or a cat, piled more coal on the fire and stuck the poker between the bars to encourage the tardy flame. She remembered the evenings when she had waited here, her heart beating like a drum in her gentle breast, waiting for the click of the gate, the familiar step on the path, and the silence came down like a curtain.

'Never again,' mocked the wind whistling round the corner. 'Never again.'

'Oh, be quiet,' cried Lily, absurdly. 'It's going to be all right.'

She pulled the curtains closer, she made tea because she couldn't stop herself from shivering. The clock ticked and she got up and put it in the kitchen where she wouldn't hear its busy heartless note. She would have gone supperless to bed, like a disgraced child, but the rain would chatter yet more incessantly on the roof. She sat on in a sort of daze, not reading, hardly even thinking. And suddenly, it happened, the gate clicked, a step came up the path.

She clutched at her heart with both hands, an instinctive gesture, because it seemed for an instant as if it would break out of her breast. She heard the gentle tap of the letter-box and she stiffened, but an instant later the steps went away in the direction of the road and the gate clicked a second time. Her breath came more evenly. She knew who it was, no snooper, no enemy to her peace, but good-hearted Mrs. Bennett leaving the cheese and bacon she brought every week, unasked. In a moment, Lily thought, she would open the door and bring them in. On such a night the porch afforded poor protection against the elements. A new thought nagged her—it had been a heavy step for Mrs. Bennett, who was a little woman as light as a leaf. Cautiously she unbarred a shutter, peeped out; sure enough the parcel lay on the step, and she realised that Mrs. Bennett would have asked her husband, George, to drop them on the porch on his way to the Bull of Basan. Nothing short of the Day of Judgment would keep him at home of an evening. Lily moved languidly into the hall. Cheese—bacon—what did they matter? But Mrs. Bennett had troubled to send them and it would look odd and ungrateful if the postman found them there next day. He still called every morning, for, if the number of anonymous letters was on the wane, there were still those who sent her tracts or warnings or spoke of the ways of Providence not being our ways and this being her last chance. There were a couple of envelopes in the box that must have come by hand while she was in the kitchen or working upstairs, but she didn't stop to take them out. There was only one letter she looked for and that, she knew, wouldn't come. She opened the door a few inches, appalled by the lashing of the rain, but as she stooped to take up the parcel a dark shadow detached itself from the clump of shadows that enveloped the porch, a hand caught her arm, a voice spoke her name.

'Miss Vane? I'm fortunate to find you . . .'

She tried to cry out, but a second hand covered her mouth, she found herself thrust backwards into the little hall. In the sitting-room a lamp was burning—she didn't kindle the gas jets, neither she nor Stephen liked them when firelight was accessible, the flames jumped fleetly from coal to coal. In that mingled light she saw a big rosy face, swags of hair under a felt hat darkened with rain. A mackintosh crackled. On the mat appeared big wet footmarks. Lily pulled away.

'You!' she panted. 'You're the one, the one at The Spinney that afternoon.'

'You don't know what you're saying,' said a deep soothing voice.

'You killed her.'

'Is that what you've been telling the police?'

'Mr. Crook,' she began. And stopped.

'Who's Mr. Crook? Now, don't be a silly girl. Tell me. Who's Mr. Crook?'

'He's a lawyer.'

The deep voice bayed into a laugh. 'He can't be a very clever lawyer if he thinks he can persuade anyone that Stephen Tate didn't kill his wife.'

'You killed her.'

'So that's what you're going to tell everyone? I was afraid you might.' The hands caught her arm, twisting it. 'There's no sense screaming, no one will hear. And you're wrong, of course. I had nothing to do with her death. Her husband killed her. And you know it. You're a silly girl, Lily Vane—I told you that before, didn't I? You've been talking to the papers.'

'No, no.' Desperately she shook her head. 'I haven't seen anyone. Only Mr. Crook.'

'You must have told someone that ridiculous story or it couldn't be printed.'

'I don't know what story you mean.'

'The story about seeing someone else at The Spinney that day.'

'I did. I saw you. Only I thought you were her. I'd never seen her, you see.'

'Till that day. You couldn't have seen me because I wasn't there. Why should I want Mrs. Tate to die?'

'Who are you? Why did you come?'

'Someone who doesn't want to get mixed up in a murder.'

Up came Lily's head. 'You're A. M. That's who you are.'

'Who's A. M.?'

'Someone Emily Tate was afraid of. Why was she afraid of you?'

'I've told you, I didn't know her. Only I can't let you go around making trouble. I've my future to consider. Not like you. You haven't any future.'

'No,' whispered Lily. 'You can't mean . . .'

'You're in love with Stephen Tate, aren't you? And he's going to die. Or even if he doesn't die he'll go to prison for years and years. He'll be an old man when he comes out, you might scarcely recognise him.' In a flash the visitor had bent double and hobbled along the floor; but the grip on Lily's arm was as firm as ever: 'Oh no, dear, you couldn't face a future like that.'

'It won't be like that,' said Lily, steadily. 'Mr. Crook would prevent it.'

'Mr. Crook! He doesn't seem to have accomplished much at present. And I don't suppose he'll really be surprised to find you couldn't face the future. No one will. You've been a bad girl, broken up a marriage, driven a man to murder—and what have you got out of it? A lifetime of regrets. Oh no, when they find you couldn't go on, no one's going to be surprised. I wonder how long it will be before anyone realises there's no sense bringing parcels any more.'

'They'll notice the milk and bread aren't being collected.' Lily forced her ashen lips to speak, struggled to subdue the shivering of her slender body.

'Not if there's a note. No Bread. No Milk. They might even think you'd run away in the darkness.'

'Why should I do that? This is the only address for me that Stephen has.'

'I've told you, it won't matter to Stephen, where you are, because he won't be able to visit you.'

'He'd know I'd never take my own life—why, it isn't mine any more, but his.'

'And his is forfeit.' The big face turned, when the head nodded approval the swags of hair bobbed up and down. 'So convenient you should have gas. Plenty of places in the country only have electricity.'

'They haven't brought electricity to Periford yet, but it's promised for next year. Then we can have television. Not that I want it really. I have a little battery set Stephen gave me . . .' The words poured out like grains of rice from a broken bag.

'Well, you won't be worrying about television or anything

else. And it's no use blaming me, you've brought this on yourself. You should have kept your mouth shut. That ridiculous story about seeing me at The Spinney.'

'How do you make me take my own life? The police are clever, they can tell suicide from murder.'

'When they find a girl in your shoes with her head in the gas oven and all the windows and doors barred they won't have much doubt.'

'How do you bolt and bar the doors and windows from the outside?'

Time, time! thought Lily, unaware that she was echoing Crook's own words. Oh Heaven, send someone. But on such a night only a man escaping from justice would be abroad, and even he would have found some shelter by now. For the rain was like a third person in The Cottage, slamming at the windows, and threatening and jeering and drowning their voices. Lily felt like someone caught in a whirlwind, battered, deprived of senses and breath.

'It's perfectly simple,' said Murder, answering her last question. 'Just put a mat against the door from the outside and when you've had time to go off take it away again and return it to the room. Don't worry too much about details, they won't be your concern.'

'Questions will be asked,' insisted Lily. 'You may have to tell them where you were this afternoon.'

'Why should anyone ask me? Anyway, there are alibis.'

'You haven't got an alibi for the day you killed Emily Tate.'

'You do get so confused, dear. I didn't kill her. Stephen did. Oh, it's all perfectly simple. Your lover's a murderer and you can't take the truth. People won't blame you, they'll understand.'

Stephen would have been amazed to see her fighting so fiercely for the life she had given to him and so couldn't yield up without a struggle. No chance against her opponent's strength, no point wasting breath crying out with nobody to hear—even if there had been a house much nearer than, in fact, there was, the storm would drown a voice however hard it cried.

'How do you persuade me to put my head in a gas oven? It'll

look strange if the police find bruises on my arms. Had you thought of that?'

'Of course,' said Murder. 'And there won't be any bruises. Look!'

'What's that?' demanded Lily, instinctively coming forward a step. She had contrived to free herself from Murder's grip, but the terrifying figure stood firmly between her and the door. 'It's a hypodermic syringe.'

'That's right. One little prick and you'll just go peacefully to sleep. That's all it is. Just a long sleep like you've often had before, only this time you won't wake up.'

Lily whirled suddenly, snatched the red-hot poker from the fire.

'Keep back,' she warned. 'I don't want to use this, but I will if I have to. It wouldn't kill you, but it would mark you for life.'

Murder was taken unawares. Poor girl, she looked perfectly insane, standing there waving that gleaming poker like a torch.

Joan of Arc en route for the asylum, thought Murder. But pokers cool quickly. Keep the girl talking, get her enthralled and watch your chance. There wouldn't be any more visitors here to-night.

'Perhaps you were in it together, you and Stephen. Perhaps you came back and killed her, and left the body for him to find. If you were really his wife you couldn't be made to give evidence, but as it is . . .'

'You forget.' Lily's breath came in sharp gasps. 'I shan't be giving evidence, shall I? I'm going to put my head in the gas oven.'

'You don't even seem to know your own mind,' Murder complained. 'An instant ago you were saying just the opposite.'

'I shall be glad to give evidence for Stephen. You think you've done a clever thing coming here to-night, but you're wrong. Because when Mr. Crook knows you were here . . .'

'Who's going to tell him? Oh, do put that thing down, dear. You don't know how silly you look.'

Lily's glance strayed automatically in the direction of the poker in her hand and in that second Murder sprang forward.

The poker clattered to the ground, where it lay burning the hearthrug; a singed smell rose on the enclosed air. Lily staggered, felt a hand push her chest and she stumbled backwards. Her head struck the corner of the chimney-piece, momentarily stunning her. Murder didn't waste a second. The loaded syringe sank into the slender white arm. Now there was no time to be lost. There was a train going south at nine-thirteen. The station was a mile away and a mile struggling against such a wind was the equivalent of two.

In the kitchen the little gas oven stood against the wall; the meter was on the wall adjacent and the beam of a torch showed that the gas supply had burned low. A single shilling was placed on the meter and Murder inserted this and three more. That should be sufficient. Back to the living-room, take the unconscious figure by the shoulders and drag her through the dark hall. The girl's heels made an untidy scuffling noise and dislodged the rug, but the rain drowned every other sound. The kitchen curtains were drawn, the windows locked. There were bars here, not shutters, but Lily had fitted squares of cardboard over the lower frames to shut out the inquisitive gaze. So much the better. Block the window with a twisted towel, take a cushion from the ancient rocking-chair (and what chi-chi that was in our day and age), plump the girl down and turn on the taps. The gas came through with a reassuring rush. The thick tan leather gloves would leave no print on gas-tap or handle and on such a night an army could have approached The Cottage unperceived. Nobody would be surprised at the lack of movement in the morning, the place was beleaguered like a fortress. Murder found a piece of paper and printed roughly on it—WARNING GAS. There had been a cheap ball-point pen lying on the dresser. Murderers have been caught before now for an instant of carelessness, using their own pens and leaving it to the police to discover the ink was a different shade or texture. There was a good deal of mud on the floor and Murder smeared some of this over the footmarks in the hall. Presently The Cottage would be dark as the oil in in the lamp burned low. There was no telephone and if anyone should come it wouldn't be surprising there would be no reply.

Slipping out by the back, whose door had been fitted with an automatic lock, Murder went away. The front door was bolted, the front gate closed. Nothing was forgotten. Nothing except what was known in the criminal world as Crook's luck, and scornfully Murder discounted that.

The Luck's owner, meantime, had seen the red light. He cursed himself in that he had put the murder weapon into the criminal's hands. He hadn't a doubt that it was going to be a race between himself and Murder, ding-dong all the way. The rain, that had been coming down pretty steadily when he reached the Sitting Duck, came driving at him as if someone stood sweeping it with a broom and flinging it against the windscreen of the big yellow car. It surged in the gutters and whirled over the low pavements. Rub-a-dub it went, like a demoniac drum. The streets were empty and no wonder. He came racing through the High Street, past the chemist's, but there was no light there, drove into Chelston where the shutters were up everywhere. He stopped at the station to make inquiries, but there was only a slow train leaving an hour hence and meandering all round the county. Quicker by road, he thought, particularly on such a night, when a train might be held up by a landslide or some other obstruction. Besides, he'd have staked the old Superb against the Golden Arrow. He shot rapid glances right and left, but saw no familiar face, only now and again someone hurried to the comfort of a brightly-lighted bar, an occasional figure, bowed under what looked like a gale-tossed mushroom, turned in thankfully at a gate. For the most part he had the road to himself, which was fortunate for would-be drivers, since he wouldn't have yielded an inch to a car flying the Royal Standard. Soon he had left Chelston and its environs far behind, was dodging through an avenue of black trees as thick as a jungle, into another town where all life existed behind glass, glimpsed bright windows, heard radios faint above the noise of the storm, all part of a world at this instant alien to himself. Rushing through a village he had never seen before, and didn't to-night, visibility being what it was, he decapitated a straying hen, made a wild swerve to avoid a questing hedgehog (dirty old man, he thought, coming out on such a night), regained his perilous path and went swooping round a corner. Even the moon and the most reckless star stayed abed to-night. The black roads unrolled, the hands of the watch tore on as fast as he. Once he lost his way and came pelting back, as furious as the rain.

He bypassed London, with its boringly conscientious policemen and senseless pedestrians who, in a common-sense state, would be made to cross the road by tunnels instead of capering about under your wheels and letting out yells and yawps like a lot of squealing pigs. Now and again people peered from their windows to see the crazy car go by, with its lunatic driver at the wheel.

'Some chaps can't love life much,' one man observed to his friend. 'Oh well, missed the war, perhaps, and feels he's been done out of something.'

In the unbuilt-up areas the Superb flew like a bird—a swan, an eagle, noble, overtaking. The darkness came closer, sky and road seemed one. He fled through traffic lights, he jumped a rash mini-car creeping out of a side road and the yell of the driver followed him like a banshee signal. A couple locked securely in a telephone booth by the roadside muttered to each other it was probably the police—meaning in their slipshod fashion that probably the police were hot in pursuit. But, though they waited, no other car came that way.

Rip Van Winkle, guessed another man, shoving open the door of The Bull in Boots at High Essen. The fountain raised by the Superb's wheels splashed his turn-ups, carried by the disrespectful wind. Presently the rain began to abate but the wind and the blackness persisted. A church clock in the market town of Harley chimed eight. Nothing but a miracle could save the situation now. Normally he made his own miracles, but sometimes even he had to give circumstances best, and that was when you looked to Providence, and, considering how few demands he made, there was a hope that to-night such a request would be honoured. It was not only his luck that was at stake, but Lily's, Lily the the golden girl, like her name-flower.

'Here, I'm going round the bend,' he discovered, alarmed. 'She's nearly as dark as the night.' Yet in his mind the image persisted.

It all depends on me, cried the posters in the last war. It all depends on me, Crook had often thought when he was well and truly up against it. But now—it all depends how much sense she has, if she refused to open a door, lean out of a window. Depends how strong her defences are, because a desperate man is like Galahad who had the strength of ten, and the same went for the opposite sex.

He spent an agonised quarter of an hour at Raymonds Cross coaxing, shoving, blaspheming the Superb out of a concealed ditch. Angels and ministers of grace, attend us, he panted. No one surfaced, but gradually, by guile, by physical force, by sheer will-power, he coaxed the big car back on to the road. After that she never put a wheel wrong. Because he couldn't let himself think what might be happening at that very instant at The Cottage, he compelled his mind down other avenues—the three chaps riding like furies to save Aix back in—what? the seventeenth century. Dirk Turpin riding to York. The chap sent to stop the Charge of the Light Brigade, who didn't make it.

It wasn't his fault or the car's that they crashed into a motor-cycle left unattended and unlighted in a dark lane. Someone came to a window and shouted and a voice yelled to him to stop. He thought madly. There was a town just ahead, and if the telephone wires weren't down a warning might be flashed to the police to look out for a madman driving a big car. He couldn't guess whether in the light from inside the chap could see her colour. He saw a side path and a signpost and decided it might prove a short cut; in any case he would bypass the town. A minute or so later he realised that, short cut or no, this road had never been intended for cars. The branches of the hedges whipped against the windows, he was in a cart-rut and out again, found himself bumping and lurching through a ploughed field; he didn't dare go slow in case she stuck in the mud, and his heart leaped again to see a gate at the far end. Praise the pigs, it wasn't padlocked, so out he leapt, a drenched hulk of a man, opened the hasp and was through. The gate he left swinging wide behind him. There were no cattle to stray and by morning someone would come along and shut it. He ran behind a farmhouse and a dog barked furiously. He heard a window go up and a voice called and someone fired an air-gun.

'Pop, pop, pop,' he called back derisively. Local loony-bin he shouldn't wonder. He slid through mud towards a black road. The Superb had been a yellow car when the run began, now she'd hold her own with any camouflaged tank, but she kept going and that was all he asked of her. It was close on nine o'clock when he reached Periford and stopped on the deserted Green in front of The Cottage. No lights were showing but he told himself that didn't mean a thing, because no lights could penetrate the shutters. There wasn't a sound but Lily wasn't like Emily, didn't want a wireless blaring twelve hours or more a day. He went charging up the path pressing the bell and turning the handle, flinging himself against the door at the same time. He felt no end of a fool when it opened smoothly and he fell like a log into the hall. A door opened and he saw that the living-room lamp was burning.

'Well, if it isn't the Bloomsbury Wonder in person,' said a voice, softly. 'I had an idea we might be seeing you to-night. Come right in and make yourself at home.'

Crook recovered his balance and turned as neatly as a taxi on its axis. Young Spence stood there, smiling at him with a sort of ferocious friendliness.

There was an instant's silence while Crook regained his breath. Then he said, with a disappointing lack of drama, 'Where is she?'

'She's—gone,' said the young man. 'I'm sorry, Crook. You're too late.'

Crook lifted his big nose and began to sniff interrogatively. 'Gas,' he announced.

'It's nothing to what it has been,' Spence reassured him. 'The back door's open and the kitchen window; this wind'll soon disperse the rest.'

Crook made a sudden plunge and went past him into the living-room where Lily had been wont to entertain her lover. Now she lay on the couch, inert, a broken flower, as some lowbrow press-man would doubtless declare.

'You brought her in here.' The words were a statement.

'You didn't expect me to leave her in the kitchen. It's colder than charity.' He saw Crook's brown eyes turn expectantly to the table. 'If you're looking for a phone there isn't one. And if you were thinking of a doctor, well, there's nothing he can do now.' He came easily down the room. 'You look as though you could use a drink,' he suggested. 'There's a bottle of whisky.' He poured a generous tot into a clean glass.

'Not my poison,' said Crook. 'There's been enough death in this case as it is.'

'Stephen Tate doesn't seem to have cared for beer. I did look. I shall be making some coffee, perhaps you'd prefer that.'

He could have attended a Fancy Dress Ball just as he was, going as the proverbial Cool Cucumber. Crook ignored the glass and bent over the girl. After an instant his head turned, he began to straighten up.

'Spence,' he said in a gentle voice that might well have alarmed a man-eater, 'this girl's breathing.'

'Well, you have to,' Spence pointed out. 'If you want to stay alive, that is.'

He shoved the glass into Crook's hand, practically closing his fingers round it. Crook lifted it like a man in a dream and drank.

'Muck!' he said, ungratefully, handing the glass back. 'Where's the nearest telephone?'

'On the Green, but I've just told you, there's nothing a doctor can do we can't do ourselves. She's not going to die, she hasn't taken in enough gas, I inspected the meter. Too bad I just missed Madam Wolf. Trouble is she's been doped before being pushed into the oven, I suppose. Look at this.'

He came round to the other side of the couch and lifted an eyelid. 'Morphia,' he said. 'A sixth or a quarter, I suppose. She wouldn't want to give her more than she had to. After all, if you're going to commit suicide by gas poisoning it's not likely you'll take a lethal dose first. Talk about two bites at a cherry. But even if she does look as though you could break her in half with one hand, she'd still be quite a job to lug down a passage if she had all her wits about her. There's a nasty bang on her head,' he continued. 'Could be she was knocked out first, then given a little prick—the syringe isn't on the premises, by the way, I've looked, unless it's in the ash can, which seems highly improbable. Much more likely to be chucked out of the train window.'

'If she came by train.'

'Oh, she came by train all right. I've had a word with the station-master. Well, I thought you'd expect it of me. I'm only acting as your stand-in, you know, and I wasn't sure I wouldn't find you on the premises.'

'Was it you who rang the Sitting Duck?'

'That's right. After I'd seen the evening edition. It did occur to me it might be part of the plot, sure way to smoke Foxy out of her hole, but they told me you'd been off as the day broke or something of the kind, so I took a chance. A second pair of hands sometimes comes in useful.'

'How can you be so sure she's all right?' inquired Crook.

'I've been here before,' said Spence simply. 'Chap I knew thought he'd take a short cut to the cemetery, and I thought it my duty to—well, deflect him. When she comes round she's going to be as sick as a dog, but everything's in readiness.'

Crook looked about him and saw the kettle puffing in the grate, the blanket, the towel, the basin.

'Coffee, that's what she'll want, everything's laid on,' young Spence continued. 'I've been trying her with whisky, but she's like you—thinks it's poison. Have another snifter, go on, faint heart never saved fair lady, and I admit I could do with one myself. Pity I missed catching X in the act,' he continued, refilling the glasses, 'but I expect our Sleeping Beauty to recognise her again, if she can't put a name to her.'

'I can do that much,' remarked Crook. 'I ought to have picked her out before this. About fourteen arrows pointing to her and I missed the lot. She's Mainprice's daughter, come scuttling back from South Africa to put the bite on Emily Tate. Full story later. Let's have your yarn now.'

'As soon as I saw the paper I drove up to the station and I was lucky; I caught a quick train, well, quick for this line, and on a night like this it was obviously safer than my little bus.

Paper had been out quite a while before I saw it, so X had a start on me. Stopped at the station at Periford to ask the old boy there had there been any passengers from Chelston and he obligingly said Yes, must have changed to the express from Barton Green. Return ticket from Chelston. I mean, he'd got the outgoing half, so whoever it was expected to come back the same way. I asked male or female and he said it was hard to tell these days but he didn't think a gentleman would be wearing a hat like that. I told him I suspected mayhem at The Cottage and he very decently lent me his bike. It's out in the cold, cold rain somewhere, probably never be fit to ride again.'

'I'll buy him a new one,' said Crook, recklessly, his eyes on the unconscious girl.

'She's coming on all right,' Spence assured him, and Crook found himself envying the capacity of the young to take everything in their stride. 'Well, but this is probably an heirloom. There can't be another one like it outside the British Museum. Well, I could see there was no sign of the Yellow Peril, and I hadn't met anyone on the way, so I began to think I might be in time. I had it all mapped out. Murder 'ud come shuffling up the path and ring the bell, and I'd fling open the door and watch her drop dead with shock. But it didn't work out that way. Of course, all the shutters were up so I couldn't tell if there were any lights burning, but I peeped through the letter-box. And then I got it. The whiff of gas. The disadvantage of putting someone's head in an oven and not being able to stop for the end of the show is that you're bound to leave some crack unblocked. This is an old place, and the doors don't fit plumb. It was that uneven kitchen door that saved her. The gas was creeping out to warn me, so round to the back I went. No shutters there, but railings and the lady had blocked the lower part of the window with cardboard or plywood or something to guard against Peeping Toms, I suppose. Still, I swung up on the sill and smashed the upper panes, and the gas came swirling out, nearly asphyxiated me, I give you my word. Not being an eel I couldn't get through the bars, but there was a useful kind of hatchet in the coal cellar, so I smashed the lock of the back door and got in. After that it was child's play. Murder didn't dare lock the kitchen door on the outside, so I just opened it, switched off the gas—she can't have had such a lot because the meter is still pretty full, it's probably the morphia that's keeping her under so long—and lugged her in here.'

'While you were at the station,' said Crook, 'did you find out what time the return train leaves?'

'Nine-thirteen.'

Crook hauled out a great turnip watch. 'She'll have gone.'

'I wouldn't count on it,' encouraged young Spence. 'They take on the mails here, don't ask me why, and everything's likely to be a bit behind time in this weather. I could hop on the station-master's bike, now you're here to hold the fort. I can phone from there just as easy as from The Green. Police, ambulance, the lot.'

Crook made one of the great gestures of his career. 'Take the Superb,' he said.

Young Spence's eyes nearly fell out. 'You mean that? I've been itching to get my hands on her wheel ever since I set eyes on her.'

'Who wouldn't?' asked Crook, reasonably, and the young man saw he meant it. 'Remember, every citizen has a right to bring a charge of murder against a fellow-citizen. And don't mention Emily Tate. Not that I need tell you what to say. Any time you're tired of being a chemist Bill and me could use you.'

Young Spence salaamed nearly to the floor; this suggestion had overcome him more than anything that had happened that day. An instant later Crook heard the front door slam, the gate swung, the Superb's engine came to life. Then smoothly, incomparably, she moved away, leaving him alone with the girl.

Perhaps, he thought in his cowardly heart, they'll get here before she comes round.

Some hopes, however pious, are destined not to be fulfilled. But Crook, who felt he'd fallen down on this case, resolved not to make any more clangers. When the moment came he coped admirably with towels, basin and all. A heartless police surgeon later told him he'd missed his vocation.

CHAPTER XI

THE rain had almost stopped when Murder left the Cottage and took the field-path to the station. The mud was thick and clogging, but you can't guard against lunatics, and there was always the chance one might be abroad, if only a doctor hauled out to visit a sick patient. She plodded in her immense shoes behind the hedges, slipping, clutching, head down. She'd timed things to a T. No point hanging about the station where an inquisitive old buffer might try and start a chat—she made the not uncommon mistake of thinking all country people yokels dying to talk to their superiors from a town—and she had stayed at The Cottage as long as seemed safe. Once through an opening in the hedge she saw a bicycle going in the opposite direction, but she didn't give that a second thought. It wasn't men on bicycles she feared. When she reached the station there was no one about. She could hear the station-master talking presumably on the telephone, so she walked on to the deserted platform and found a minute shed, marked Ladies Waiting Room, with some extremely primitive toilet facilities adjoining. Into these she vanished, planning to reappear only when she heard the train come in. Probably no one would bother to clip her ticket here, and there'd be a collector on the train, she supposed. It was a bit of luck that no one else was travelling.

After a while she realised the train was late, and she had a pang of terror in case she'd dozed off for five minutes or something and it had come and gone. But a sack she had noticed when she came on to the dark wet platform was still there, so it was just a question of the train being held up. She crouched over a few miserable sticks and crumbs of coal in the tiny grate, but there was no warmth to be had from them. Still, it gave her a good opportunity to keep her back to the door in case anyone else should turn up, and if she heard feet or voices she could go into retirement again. The station-master hadn't witnessed her arrival, and she could possibly slip on to the train unnoticed. Once aboard she didn't mind who spoke to her; she knew that in England people can sit next to you on public transport for a couple of hours and be uncertain at the end of that time if you're man, woman or chimpanzee.

Her clock ticked on, no one arrived. The station-master was probably having a snack in his little hole; she began to shiver—well, rain and wind and no heat from the fire, what could you expect? She found herself wondering how long a young person would take to die of gas poisoning. There had been a case in the papers recently concerning a child left alone, who had foolishly turned a gas tap and not known how to turn it off again, who had succumbed in a little more than half an hour. She looked once more at her watch. Four shillings' worth of gas would surely have evaporated by morning, and no one would disturb Lily before then. She thought it might have been a good idea to leave a note, but an unsigned note always aroused suspicion and Lily might have a particular signature. It had been risky enough, probably, to put the warning on the door, but from what she had heard of the girl it seemed such a step would be in character.

At last, peering through the small stained window, she saw the signal had dropped. She snapped her big handbag open and dabbed a powder puff over her big high-coloured face. The instant the train drew up she would dart out.

At the same instant a car drew up outside the station. Someone hopped out and went into the station-master's office. She drew a breath of relief. By the time the train came in they'd probably be deep in conversation and then there were the mails to be attended to. It was a matter of seconds now.

No train surely had ever taken so long to reach its destination. She could hear the distant rumble, stood taut as a runner. Then the station-master appeared and opened the waiting-room door.

'Didn't see you arrive, miss,' he said. 'Ticket, please.'

She wrenched it out of her purse and offered it to him. He turned it over, scanning the date on the back.

'It's in order,' she said impatiently.

'No change,' he said. 'Through train. Bit late because of the weather.'

She half-snatched it from him. 'Plenty of time,' he said, opening the door slowly. 'Oh, beg pardon, sir.' This was to a young man who sprang out of the darkness like a Jack from its box. He went out, closing the door. The newcomer leaned against it and folded his arms.

'Will you kindly allow me to get on that train?' panted Murder.

'No hurry, Mrs. Rodding,' said the young man. 'You won't be travelling on this train. They're laying on special transport for you.'

'You're mad or drunk,' she said. The darkness, the mist, her own heart's fear, seemed to throw up a sort of cloud through which it was difficult to see his face. 'I have my ticket . . .'

'I've just told you, you won't be wanting it.'

'I don't know who you are . . .'

'Sure? Take a good look. Spence is the name. I'm running the chemist's shop at Little Wyvern, the one that used to belong to Emily Tate. Don't tell me you don't remember Emily.'

She leaned forward and knocked imperiously on the glass window.

'What's that for?' asked Peter. 'Going to give me in charge? You'll have your chance in a minute. The police are on their way.'

'The police?'

'Crook's up at The Cottage,' he told her. 'He sent me down to detain you. Lent me his own car, if you can believe it.'

The station-master came back. 'Is the lady travelling?' he inquired.

'Yes,' shouted Mrs. Rodding.

'No,' said Peter Spence.

One of the passengers, an ambitious young man who'd had a wasted twenty-four hours on a particularly unrewarding assignment from his paper, smelt news. In a trice he was out of the train and had joined the little group. Always follow a hunch was his motto, and if he lost this train there was still time to be back in Fleet Street by morning. It involved a two-hour wait at two o'clock in the morning on a branch line, but what of it? He'd long ago learned to sleep standing on his feet, like a horse.

'Battle, murder or sudden death?' he offered, pleasantly, pushing forward, his overnight bag slung on his shoulder.

'Certainly the last two,' Peter assured him. 'Quite probably the first as well.'

'Station-master,' insisted Mrs. Rodding. 'I wish to catch that train.'

The engine driver leaned out of his cab and bawled. The station-master bawled back. Then he turned to the young man.

'Are you the police, sir?'

'Plain clothes branch,' agreed young Spence, obligingly. He had both Murder's wrists in his grasp, but he cunningly shifted it to free one hand and haul a bit of pasteboard out of his pocket.

'Nonsense,' cried Mrs. Rodding. 'He's a chemist.'

'Whizzo,' said the pressman. 'Dumb Crambo up to date.' Already he had his greyhound nose in the air and was sniffing about as if he expected to smell blood, powder, and the peculiar smell of Authority all mixed together. One or two heads appeared at train windows.

'Good old England,' said a voice. 'Not so much as a bloody cup of tea. What's going on?'

The station-master was looking perturbed. 'You never said you were the police, sir,' he remarked reprovingly.

'He's not,' yelled Mrs. Rodding.

A bicycle came splashing through the sodden lane and an instant later a middle-aged man came on to the platform.

'My son-in-law,' said the station-master. 'Sergeant Bennett. Mind you, he's not on duty really, but . . . Well, murder's murder, but naturally you like to favour your own family.'

'The police are like doctors, on duty twenty-four hours a day,' capped Peter Spence. 'Officer, I wish to give this lady in charge for wilful murder.'

Sergeant Bennett looked round as if he expected the corpse to drop down the chimney or pop up through the floor.

'Where's the body, sir?'

'Up at The Cottage. Mr. Crook's standing guard.'

'That Crook?' said the young pressman. He turned to the sergeant. 'Borrow your bike?'

'That's enough of borrowed bikes,' broke in the station-master. 'Mine's still to come.'

'It's being looked after,' Spence assured him. 'Crook lent me his car.'

The pressman saw the opportunity and jumped for it like a rabbit going through a hole in a wall.

'Could be he'd like it back,' he offered.

'Why not?' said young Spence. 'I've promised to hold the fort till he turns up.' The pressman disappeared like a genie. Spence shrieked directions after him.

'I'll find it,' promised the young man, confidently. And he would, too, if he had to press a button and say, Hey, presto! 'Tell him the earth's stopped,' Spence yelled, louder than before.

The engine driver, despairing of getting any sense out of anyone, released his brake and the train jolted slowly out of the station.

'Now,' said Sergeant Bennett, 'what's all this?'

'You'll soon know. The main body of troops are up at The Cottage now.'

'I thought, Bert,' said his father-in-law with dignity, 'seeing you represent the law here you should be on the scene. Murder's no joke.'

'You can say that again,' said young Spence.

'I know nothing about a murder,' insisted Mrs. Rodding.

'It's news to me that gas can turn itself on, and no one I ever met put her head into an oven by accident.'

Bert said weightily, 'There's suicide, sir.'

'Of course it's suicide, if that's what's happened,' Mrs. Rodding declared.

'Only there doesn't seem any motive, now Mr. Crook's on the case. Still, we'll wait for the young lady's story.'

Mrs. Rodding's big face seemed to cave in like a pudding when someone bashes it with a spoon.

'You said she was dead,' she spluttered.

'Well, she ought to be, only they say God's on the side of the big battalions, and if you can find a bigger one than Arthur Crook just point it out to me.'

The telephone rang and the station-master went to answer it. The three in the waiting-room stood like mutes until Mrs Rodding said, 'If she's not dead what happens to your murder charge?'

'No thanks to you if she isn't,' said young Spence, 'and Emily Tate is—don't forget Emily.'

The station-master came back. 'They're sending reinforcements, Bert,' he said. 'In the meantime, hold the lady.'

He had a dreamy look in his eye. He was seeing the local Press —Station-master's son-in-law in Murder drama. Lucky he'd thought of ringing Bert. He'd never had a murder in all his years in the Force.

Young Spence spoke the last word before the police arrived. 'You're lucky really,' he said. 'Not just because if Lily Vane had died it 'ud have meant the rope, but I wouldn't give much for your chances of an easy death if Stephen Tate had got you when he's returned to circulation.'

Lily Vane spent the night at the local hospital, taken thither in an ambulance. A police car collected Mrs. Rodding on suspicion and housed her for the night in the local gaol. It wasn't possible to establish telephonic communication with Chelston that night because of the havoc wrought by the storm, but the authorities of the G.P.O. are no slouches and as soon as it was light chaps would be repairing the damage. Already the storm was blowing itself out.

The woman fought like a tiger-cat for her liberty. 'You can't hold me,' she insisted. 'You've nothing against me except a trumped-up story by a man who wouldn't care how unscrupulous he was if it would get his client off.'

'As a citizen,' Crook assured her, 'I can bring a murder charge.'

'You've just said Miss Vane isn't dead.'

'Someone murdered Mrs. Tate. Miss Vane will identify you as the woman she saw at The Spinney that afternoon.'

'Coached by you,' began Mrs. Rodding furiously.

'I haven't had a chance of coaching her,' demurred Crook. 'You saw to that. By the way, what happened to the syringe?'

'The . . . ?'

'You heard. Still got it in your bag? It wasn't in the Cottage. Or did you shed it by the wayside?'

They found it in her bag. 'That proves nothing,' she said.

'Habit of yours to carry a syringe around with you? Anyway, there's the evidence of the note on the door. Remember—WARNING GAS. Like to show the officer your fountain pen?'

'Certainly. And he can testify that that note was written with a ball-pen . . .' She stopped, arrested by those popping brown eyes.

'So he can,' agreed Crook. 'How come you knew, though? It's the oldest trick in the world,' he added before she could think up a reply. 'Either they use their own and it can be proved there isn't a pen on the premises with that colour ink or else they're so keen to show it wasn't theirs they tie the noose with their own hands. I'll be round to-morrow with Miss Vane, if they'll let her out. And meantime,' he added in his unchivalrous fashion that was proof in itself that he'd never earned the right to wear the old school tie, 'you think up a good reason why you should have travelled to Periford on a day even a self-respecting duck would have stopped at home. And it better be good.'

'Wouldn't you know the one time I landed a scoop the telephones would be down?' groaned the Press representative, but Crook said, 'Oh, you'll have Fleet Street humming just the same. If you can't use the phone nor can anyone else.'

The two young men travelled back on the last train of the day that came through at midnight and stopped at Periford, no one could tell you why. The news 'ud be too late to make the first editions, but it would be all over the midday papers. 'And it won't lose much in the telling, not if that young chap has anything to do with it,' prophesied Crook. The station-master said he and his wife had a spare-room he could have and welcome. They'd brought his bicycle back on the Superb, not much the worse for wear.

When the police went over The Cottage with a toothcomb they found Mrs. Rodding's fingerprints on two of the shillings she had pushed into the gas meter. She had found it difficult to manipulate them in her thick gloves and she had pulled them off for a moment, and even she couldn't talk herself out of that one.

'When did you tumble to her?' young Spence asked Crook when the latter came back to Little Wyvern.

'A lot later than I should have done,' returned Crook, grimly. 'If it hadn't been for you it 'ud have been a case of The angels in Heaven are singing to-day, Here's Lily, here's Lily, here's Lily. Well, work it out for yourself. We were looking for a big woman, middle-aged, rosy-faced, fair hair going grey, surfacing round about the time Louisa Mainprice died. And here she was in the middle of the picture. It had to be someone who knew the neighbourhood and knew that 24 Curtonbridge Street was an accommodation address. It had to be someone connected in some fashion with Emily Tate's past, and it wasn't likely it was a new acquaintance, because if so you'd have been on to it— any little matter of passing dangerous drugs or anything of that kind. It was someone who could demand a sizeable price for silence, and the payments couldn't go through the books. Of course the pension to Mainprice and later to Louisa could be set against expenses, but the Inland Revenue authorities would have woke up in a hurry if she'd tried to put down regular payments to Mainprice's daughter whom she'd never officially seen. It was Mrs. Crabbe who put me on to it in the end. She said the Mainprice girl had a suitcase with A. S. on it, and had explained she hadn't bothered to change the initials, but her new plastic handbag was marked A. R.'

'And you started doing a bit of arithmetic . . .'

'When did Mrs. Rodding surface at Chelston? A few months previously, just about the time Emily Tate began making her mysterious payments. An envelope is found at The Spinney addressed to 24 Curtonbridge Street, but the proprietor says she doesn't recall any A. M. Now there should have been five letters addressed to A. M., so it's a bit odd that she doesn't remember them. She recognised her clients all right, knew which were the ones who were playing with fire, and an envelope containing a hundred pound notes is a sizeable concern. No, she told the police, no one called A. M. ever came here, I'm pretty certain. And she was right in the sense that they weren't called for.'

'I still don't get it,' Spence admitted. 'Say Emily had destroyed the will and the Mainprices knew it, how did Ayleen hope to prove such a thing?'

'From all I've heard about old Mainprice he knew how to look after Number One. I fancy there was a little slip of paper somewhere with Emily Tate's signature to it. He wouldn't really have been safe without something of the kind. And she wouldn't dare refuse to sign it. Remember after Louie died how Emily went beetling down dead keen to rummage among the dear departed's papers? I bet that's what she was looking for, not realising that Mamma had probably got it safely banked for the benefit of the next generation. And when Ayleen turned up she must have felt at the end of her tether.'

'That's what she said in her letter,' remembered young Spence.

'A letter she never wrote to her husband. No, if I were defending Mrs. Rodding I'd plump for self-defence, and it wouldn't surprise me if that was a true bill. We've wondered all along why it should be Emily Tate that was murdered. Ayleen was drawing a nice little nest-egg each month, why chuck it away?'

'Meaning that Emily asked her over to cut her throat! Oh come, Crook, murder's not a game.'

'Know the most dangerous criminal there is? The murderer who's got away with it the first time. For one thing, it gives him a swollen head. Here's Little Me bamboozled the whole police force. I'm omnipotent, no one can catch me. And then, when opportunity offers, he strikes again.'

'Which was the first murder?' asked Peter Spence, carefully.

'Don't it strike you that Daddy died very conveniently just

when he was about to hand over her inheritance to someone else?
And just after his *tête-à-tête* with Mainprice?'

'Her own father?' Spence sounded horrified.

'A scheming mischievous rather unpleasant old gentleman with
a perverted sense of humour,' Crook corrected him. 'What do we
know about him? He wouldn't take his daughter into partnership,
he only married in middle life to get a son and instead he got two
daughters. He schemed and angled to get Tate for a son-in-law,
and it 'ud be quite in accord with everything we know about
him if at the eleventh hour he decided to give his son-in-law the
shop. No one could stop him under our asinine laws. Tate, who's
one of nature's sucking-doves, never really saw through him,
but he said one thing I don't forget. He liked reciting the cursing
psalms. If you remember those . . .'

Young Spence nodded. 'Not exactly Daddy Christmas. Still,
murder's a bit steep, wouldn't you say?'

'Parents have a habit of underestimating their children. He
was playing with dynamite if he'd only guessed. We have Tate's
word for it that she lived, ate, breathed the shop, and now by a
nasty death-bed trick Daddy's going to cheat her of it. Women
are amazing creatures, as you'll learn. They can persuade themselves black's white if black is what they need. Wouldn't surprise
me if Emily Tate felt perfectly justified in putting Paid to the old
boy's account, and outraged when Mainprice challenged her.'

'How'd he know?'

'I suppose while Emily was occupied being so attentive to dear
old Dad—no one was ever allowed to be alone with him, remember,
except Mainprice that one afternoon. The assistant would have a
duplicate key to the drugs cupboard. Maybe when the old man
died so conveniently he had his suspicions and started checking
quantities. Remember, Emily would be taken by surprise, she
wouldn't have a chance to make up a yarn, she'd have to decide
what to do in a matter of seconds. I dare say if she could have
sent him to join Papa she wouldn't have hesitated, but there was
no knowing he hadn't confided in Mrs. M., and there was that
private conversation which could now cover anything Mainprice chose to tell. There was no old Mr. Purdy to deny it. No,

she was in a cleft stick, and personally I'd say she was as guilty as hell, otherwise why not tell him to get the police on the blower? From that moment on she was like a prisoner with a ball and chain on his leg. Old Mainprice could call the tune. Mind you, he'd probably show some discretion. A woman who doesn't stop short of putting her father underground has to be respected the same way you'd respect a cobra, but he's made for life and he knows it. So—as long as the old man lives she's got to toe the line. It wasn't generosity that made her go on paying the pension but fear of the old lady's tongue. The old man, I understand, had lost the power of speech, but Louie was very much all there.'

'And then Louie dies of a broken heart . . .'

'Didn't I tell you?' said Crook. 'She died of an overdose. And she died the night after Emily Tate had been paying a visit, brought a nice fat chicken and a bunch of flowers, well, p'raps the chicken wasn't that day, I forget, but Madam Mainprice ate like a queen and well she could afford to. Only once she's gone there's no one to call the tune—that's how Emily argues—and she's been dancing pretty strenuously for the better part of ten years.'

'Well, but look here,' protested Peter Spence, 'you're not telling me the old lady would take anything dear Emily mixed for her.'

'Not blooming likely,' agreed Crook. 'She took the stuff herself hours after Emily had gone home. But—work it out this way. Here are the two tubes of pills—the aspirins or what-have-you and the sleeping tablets. Emily's only got to say, "'Scuse me one minute while I powder my nose or fetch the letters or get you a clean hanky," and transfer a couple of the sleeping pills to the other tube. According to Mrs. Crabbe they were similar in appearance, though the tubes themselves were labelled carefully enough. Sooner or later—and a day this way or that don't make much difference—Louisa's going to want a couple of aspirins, and she's going to take the top two from the tube. Of course, there's a hundred-to-one chance she could drop the tube and spill the contents, but that's a chance anyone has to take. It so happened she felt a bit done up after her conversation with Emily and took them the same night. Emily's in clover. The Lord Chief Justice himself couldn't prove her guilty; what the Courts want is proof, not horse-sense.'

'You have to admit she's a trier,' suggested Peter Spence. 'First Dad, then Louisa Mainprice, and then, according to you, Mrs. Rodding.'

'Well,' said Crook reasonably, 'can you think of any other reason for inviting a lady scorpion to visit you in your own house?'

'What was she going to use this time? Another cup of cold pizen?'

'Mrs. Rodding 'ull tell us that,' asserted Crook, confidently.

Mrs. Rodding did.

CHAPTER XII

A FAMOUS newspaper put up the money for Mrs. Rodding's defence. Crook's melodramatic manner of dealing with crime had helped to make it front page news, and a man called Scrymgeour went to the prison to get the accused story.

She said:

'Mrs. Tate asked me to come and see her at The Spinney to discuss a matter of business. She said we should be more private there than if she came to Curtonbridge Street, and as it was a Thursday when both our shops were closed for the afternoon—(I reopened later when the papers came in and she for prescriptions)—we could talk at leisure. I went by bus and arrived about one-twenty or one twenty-five. Mrs. Tate hadn't been back long, she had taken off her hat and gloves, but still wore her outdoor coat. The wireless was playing. She took me into the living-room but we had hardly begun to talk when someone rang the front-door bell. She said she was expecting no one and if we took no notice whoever it was would go away. About a minute later the back-door bell rang, and she said she would go into the kitchen and would peep through the curtains. She disappeared and after a few seconds it occurred to me she might be laying some sort of trap. I called out, "What's happening?" and she called back, "Oh, it was a boy with onions. He's gone now. The kettle's boiling and I'm just going to make a cup of tea." I didn't trust her not to put something into the cup along with the milk and sugar and I called, "I'll come and join you." She said, "Yes, it's the end of the passage."

'To reach the kitchen you went down the passage and turned right into a tiny lobby with a door on either side. The one on the left opened into a glass cupboard, the one on the right, that was covered by a long curtain, shut off a flight of steps leading to a disused cellar. As I turned into the lobby Mrs. Tate came rushing out of the kitchen and collided with me. I moved instinctively to the right and she pushed me violently against the curtain. I then realised that the door behind the curtain had been folded back against the wall. Clearly she meant me to crash down the stone steps, where I should probably have broken my neck. In any case, she didn't intend me to leave The Spinney alive. As we had never had any open communication no one would think of looking for me there, and as the cellar hadn't been used for years a body could be hidden there indefinitely. At that time she didn't realise Mr. Tate was planning to leave her. I snatched at the curtain and was lucky enough to get a bit of a grip on the framework. Mrs. Tate was like a madwoman; she clawed at my hand and did her utmost to overset me. Fortunately I'm a good deal larger and heavier than she and I managed to wrench myself clear. She was wearing a scarf round her neck and I caught one end of it so suddenly that she spun round, and I regained my balance and caught the other end. I pulled, to make her stop her attack, and suddenly she crumpled up. I thought at first she had fainted. When I found she was dead I was appalled. Of course, I know now I should have telephoned for the police at once, but I suppose I lost my head.'

('And, of course, the police might have asked a few awkward questions,' supplemented Crook. 'It's never easy to talk yourself out of blackmail.')

Questioned as to the nature of the business that had brought her to The Spinney, she said:

'Years ago my father did Mrs. Tate a great service. If it hadn't been for him she would have lost the shop altogether, and might well have stood her trial for murder. My father knew that Mr. Purdy intended to change his will and make his son-in-law his heir, but before he could put this into effect he died. My father became suspicious and examined the contents of the drugs cupboard; he thought it probable that Mr. Purdy had had an overdose. Naturally he didn't want to be involved in a scandal—he was an elderly man and he had to think of himself and my mother—and they came to an agreement under which he stayed on as manager, but he had a document signed by Emily Tate that would have proved highly dangerous to her if it ever became public property. I wasn't concerned with the morality of that, what's done can't be undone and he had the future to consider.'

No, she said, she hadn't known any of this at the time; she was out of touch with her father, who was one of the old-fashioned Sabbatical Christians. (Heart of gold and about as melting, was Crook's pithy comment.) She had married a Mr. Smith some years before and gone with him to South Africa, but the marriage had turned out badly, Mr. Smith had behaved with great cruelty and finally she had left him for the protection of a Mr. Rodding, whose name she had thenceforth used. She wrote to explain the situation to her parents, and received a bitter letter from her father telling her never to return during his lifetime.

'My mother and I kept up a correspondence,' she went on, 'and after my father's death she wrote to me to come home. She said she would be able to leave me a little legacy and she would like to tell me about it. Mr. Rodding had died by now, he was an elderly man; we had had a little store at Durban, but it never made very much money for us and I was glad to sell up and come home. I had to wait some time for a passage and when I did get back I found my mother had died also. She had left a letter for me with Mrs. Crabbe; it was addressed to Mrs. Smith as that was my legal name, but I never used it after I left my husband. No, I never changed my name by deed poll.'

Mrs. Mainprice had left a letter explaining the peculiar circumstances and enclosing Emily's signed 'confession', but this Mrs. Rodding was not able to produce. She said that after Emily's death she had destroyed anything that might link her name with the dead woman. She had laid her plans with some cunning. Needing some sort of job, she had heard of the shop in Curtonbridge Street and had leased it from old Mr. Samuelson. From that address she had written to Emily, suggesting that she should sent an appropriate sum of money to A. M., c/o 24 Curtonbridge Street.

'You mean that Mrs. Tate never knew you as Mrs. Rodding?'

'No. That was why I used my girlhood's initials. She had never met me and if she did come to the shop I saw no advantage in her recognising me. After all, she had proved herself ruthless in getting her own way, and she might prove dangerous to me, too. She brought the money each month herself in a parcel, always on a Thursday afternoon. The shop was shut but she brought it to the side door. She never gave her name, or stopped for more than a moment.'

'So that when she saw you at The Spinney it was a considerable shock to her?'

'I suppose it was. But we never really had time to get to any conclusion. She had written this letter about being at the end of her tether and in the first half, that I destroyed, she asked me to bring the paper with me. She wanted to buy it back for a lump sum. When I saw that she was dead I meant to slip out and go straight back to Chelston. No one would connect me with her death, and I was fairly sure she had never spoken of me to anybody. Then Miss Vane came to the front door. I thought if I didn't move she would presently go away, but I had forgotten about the wireless. That showed her, I suppose, there must be someone on the premises. I was afraid she meant to stay there all the afternoon, so I opened the door a crack meaning to say it was no good waiting—without letting her see me properly—but she came bursting in, calling me Mrs. Tate and telling me who she was. Seeing she had never met Emily I thought I might turn this visit to my advantage, so I got rid of her quickly. Of course it changed my plans. If the news went round that Mrs. Tate was dead, and it wasn't a natural death, this girl would realise I was the last person to see her alive. I imagined that the Press would make it obvious that the woman she saw hadn't been Emily Tate. But if Mrs. Tate simply disappeared, then her husband and the girl might think it was on their account. I left the half-sheet of paper, pushed a few things into a bag, and managed to get the body into the car. I could drive, fortunately, and I knew at that hour on a Thursday it wasn't likely there would be many people about. The rest of the story you know already.

I weighted her handbag and little suitcase with stones, they're somewhere at the bottom of the river, which is very deep there. I had noticed the car dump on a walk one afternoon, and it seemed as safe a place as any to ditch the car. I removed the number-plates, and tried to make it look derelict. In the sort of weather we were having it might be weeks before anyone noticed it. It was self-defence,' she added, passionately. 'I never meant to kill her, I had no motive.'

'Not a nice woman all the same,' Crook commented to young Spence. 'She'd have left the body like a shot and seen Tate sent to chokey for life and probably lost no sleep at all. And even she can't pretend the attack on Lily Vane was an accident. If she'd known about me,' he added, 'my non-existent heirs could have started claiming life assurance before long I wouldn't wonder. Mrs. Crabbe would have recognised her, wonder if she'd have had a shot at her, too. Oh well, it's an axiom that one murder nearly always leads to another. All the same,' he added un-expectedly, 'you've cause to be grateful to the lady.'

'Me?' exclaimed young Spence. 'What on earth did she do for me?'

'You can't bring non-existent evidence into court. There's no proof that Emily's confession ever existed, beyond her word. If it could have been shown that she poisoned her old man—well, under British law a criminal can't profit by his crime. She couldn't have claimed the shop and it would have gone to the old man's next-of-kin, and that's Beattie Baynes, and you could die on her doorstep in a blizzard before she'd let you sit free of charge in her hall. And where would you have been then?'

Young Spence looked down from his considerable height and smiled.

'Little Wyvern's not the world,' he said. 'Mind you, I don't deny it would have been a blow, but Harry and I would have set up somewhere else. You cannot keep a squirrel on the ground and when it's a pair of them and one of them Harry, you'd be a blooming fool to try.'

He bounded off as briskly as his precious squirrel to collect his mate, leaving Crook to look after him a bit wistfully. He wasn't a man who bothered much about advancing years, but sometimes he found himself envying The Wandering Jew or Rip Van Winkle, who'd gone on indefinitely. He couldn't believe a time would ever come when he'd be tired of life.

The door of his flat reopened suddenly and young Spence stuck his head in.

'Hope the Tates send you a nice bit of wedding cake,' he said. 'Harry's making ours now—what you want done right you do yourself—p'raps you'll get the ring this time—or am I thinking of Christmas puddings?'

Stephen went one better than sending Crook a slice of wedding cake. After his release he turned up at Bloomsbury Street with a sizeable cheque. ('Here, that's too much,' protested Crook. 'All the gold of Araby wouldn't be enough,' was Stephen's retort.) And a request to the Bloomsbury Wonder to give the bride away. He was taking his job in the north and seemed quite calm about it.

'People don't remember for long,' he said, 'and it's not as though I killed Emily. Bit disappointing for them really, I suppose.'

On the day Lily became Mrs. Stephen Tate she confessed. 'Of course, I was terrified, but even when I was facing her with the red-hot poker I knew somehow it would be all right, because I had you on my side, and you never let your clients down.'

'With a faith like that you didn't need me,' said Crook. 'You can work your own miracles.'

A few months later business took him into the neighbourhood, and he stopped in the High Street. Emily Purdy's demure chemist's shop was scarcely recognisable. Young Spence and his bride had taken over the adjoining premises and the whole thing was going great guns. When he spoke Crook saw he had put the whole past out of mind, Stephen, Emily, the girl whose life he had been instrumental in saving. To hear him talk was like watching a firework display. As Crook turned to go he said, 'Have you heard the latest? No one seems keen to buy The Spinney, but the new TV set-up beyond Huntmere has rented it for their latest picture.

They're doing a re-hash of the Crippen case, and they're calling it Cellar's Market. How about that for a last word?'

'I could think of a better one,' said Crook sedately, 'but there's a lady present.'

And humming his favourite hymn-tune, 'A few more years shall roll,' he hopped into the Superb and rushed away.

>>> If you've enjoyed this book and would like to discover more great vintage crime and thriller titles, as well as the most exciting crime and thriller authors writing today, visit: >>>

The Murder Room
Where Criminal Minds Meet

themurderroom.com

9 781471 910180